QUEEN OF RUIN

KINGMAKER TRILOGY
BOOK 2

PAULA DOMBROWIAK

KINGMAKER BOOK TWO

QUEEN
OF *Ruin*

PAULA DOMBROWIAK

By: Paula Dombrowiak
Copyright © 2024 Paula Dombrowiak

Cover Image: Stock Photo
Cover Design: Lori Jackson www.lorijacksondesign.com
Editor: Hart to Heart Edits
Proofreader: Katy Nielsen

www.pauladombrowiak.com

CONTENTS

For those who think history is sexy.

PROLOGUE

Four Years Earlier

Evangeline

"What can I get you?" I ask from behind the counter, simultaneously grabbing a muffin and placing it on a plate while I wait for the customer to answer.

Rubbing my hands on my apron, I barely look up to register who I'm speaking with, and when I do, I notice an older man with dark, wavy hair, and eyes a color I can't discern. He's wearing a suit, not something I see often in here. A line starts to form behind him, and I remember the other drinks I need to get started on.

Pressing the grounds, I flip on the espresso machine while grabbing a cup for another drink.

"Just a black coffee." The man shrugs.

"Taking it easy on me," I jest, raising my eyebrows, because otherwise why would he have been taking his time to order if it was just going to be a black coffee?

"You look busy," he observes, handing me his card.

"Tap it here." I point to the card reader.

He laughs, embarrassed, taking the card back and

touching it to the reader. "I can never get used to these things."

"It's okay, there are a lot of things I can't seem to get a handle on either," I mention before starting on the backlog of drinks. I grab a paper cup, pour black coffee into it for him, snap on the top, and hand it to him at the end of the counter.

"Thanks." He grabs hold of it and puts a twenty-dollar bill in the tip jar which I'm not shy about accepting as I nod appreciatively at him.

I sort through the rest of the drinks and glance at my open book on the counter, trying to get in a few extra minutes of studying before I have to leave for class.

"Where's Natalie?" my manager, Michelle, asks.

"I don't know." I'm done covering for Natalie because there are only so many excuses I can make, and if she thinks I'm sharing the tips with her, she's crazy.

Michelle huffs and then picks up taking orders at the register while I finish the rest of the drinks. The morning rush dissipates just in time for me to leave. Checking the clock, I realize I only have fifteen minutes to get to class. I rush out the door, juggling my drink, when I smack right into some-one, coffee spilling over my books as they crash to the pavement.

"Jesus, I'm sorry." The man kneels to help me with my things and I notice his shiny dress shoes, and the hem of neatly pressed trousers splattered with coffee.

"No, it's my fault." I look up at him to make sure the rest of his expensive-looking suit isn't tarnished. I push a few papers into my bag and shake my hair out of my face.

We both stand, and I notice he's holding my book, looking at it with an interesting expression. "Collective works of Ralph Waldo Emerson," he observes.

I realize he's the man who just ordered a black coffee. Taking the book from him, I toss my now empty cup of coffee in the nearby trash.

"Yeah," I laugh. "It's so boring."

"You think Emerson is boring?" He sounds appalled.

"I mean, half the time I have no idea what he's trying to say." I stuff the book back in my bag and hoist it over my shoulder.

"Emerson is a fascinating historical figure! I mean, he was compared to Nietzsche, and supported the Transcendental movement with the likes of Walt Whitman. Boring, no, no, no. You cannot think he's boring," he exclaims, and I now realize his eyes are a complicated color, and they light up while he talks about Emerson, trying to convince me to like the man, not just his poetry.

"Are you a professor?" It would be just like me to put my foot in my mouth and end up having him as a teacher next semester. He looks to be the right age, maybe somewhere in his mid to late forties.

"No," he laughs. "I'm giving a lecture to the student senate, and hopefully they don't mind if I throw in a little Emerson."

"What does Emerson have to do with politics?"

"Everything," he declares, and his smile is so inviting, so genuine, that I'm eager to understand more.

"I wish I had time to ask you to explain that to me, since I'm about to take a test on Emerson, but I don't have time," I apologize.

He holds his coffee out to me. "I didn't drink any. I was waiting for it to cool off."

"I don't take drinks from strangers." I lift an eyebrow. "Even handsome ones," I add.

"Oh, um," he scratches his head and I'm immediately embarrassed for misreading his kindness. "I wasn't trying to…. Old habit of charming voters," he stumbles over his words.

He's definitely charming, even if he doesn't mean to be. "A politician huh?"

"Afraid so." He looks around the small courtyard that connects the student dorms to the cafeteria, and then points to a shady spot under a tree where a man who looks completely out of place is standing with a watchful eye. "Security," he explains, "so don't try anything or he'll tackle you."

I laugh, holding a hand to my face. "I'm sorry, I'm so late for class. Good luck with your lecture."

I race off toward the English building. Once I'm across the street, I turn to see if he's still there, but he's walking in the opposite direction with the security detail at his side.

When I get to the classroom, I pull on the door, but it doesn't budge - locked. Looking through the small window I can see everyone in their seats, pencils up, and heads down.

"Shit!"

I raise my hand to knock on the door, but hesitate, because it will get the attention of the whole class. Continuing to stare through the window, Professor Abbott happens to look up and see me. When he gets 'the look', I can already tell he's not going to let me in.

He's a tall man with blond hair and glasses too small for his face.

"You're late," he announces, peering at me over his spectacles.

"I know, I was leaving work and ran into someone..."

"Stopping to talk to your friends is no excuse for being late."

"No, I literally ran into someone on the street, my coffee went all over my book and papers," I explain, but all he does is shake his head and I don't know if he believes me or not.

"Did you know today was the test?" he asks.

"Yes, but..."

"Then you should have left work earlier to account for any mishaps."

"Natalie never showed up. I had to finish my shift." I pull

out my book. "Look at my book, if you don't believe me." I hold it out for him, the pages discolored and wrinkled with coffee stains.

"I'm sorry, Ms. Bowen," he says, pushing his glasses back up his nose. "The rules are you have to be in your seat when class begins. I can't give you a pass when everyone else was here on time."

Shoving the book back in my bag I let out a defeated breath.

"Is there any way I can make it up?" I plead.

"I don't give makeup tests unless you're sick," he continues, "and you look very healthy to me." Whether he means to or not, the way his eyes slide over my body makes me uncomfortable.

"What will an incomplete on the test do to my grade?" I inquire, because I need to keep my grade point average for my scholarship money to come through.

"You can see me after class and I can look up your grades," he offers, "but if my recollection is accurate, you don't have a stellar grade to begin with."

Maybe if Professor Abbott wasn't such a boring teacher I'd be doing better. Between the cafe in the morning and waitressing at night, I barely have time to study.

As soon as the door shuts behind him, I slump against the hallway wall and slide down until my butt hits the rough carpet. Why does everything have to be so hard for me? Tears prick at the back of my eyes, and I am defenseless against them.

Pulling my knees up, I rested my forehead against them.

I wanted to be Melinda Carleton, the investigative journalist who won a Pulitzer for her Russian spy piece, but all of that felt like grasping at stars – so far away that I'd never be able to reach. I began to feel resentful of girls like Natalie who miss work, and even if she gets fired, it's no real consequence, because it was just extra money for her. For me, it would determine whether I had a place to live next semester, or whether I could afford my meal plan.

Lifting my head, I wipe the tears away, not sure if that made me feel better or not. I've learned to give myself some grace for the occasional emotional breakdown. When my vision comes back into focus, I see a flyer taped to the wall - Student Government Welcomes Distinguished Speaker Senator Kerry Walker (R) Virginia.

A senator? The man with a nice smile and a slight southern accent was Senator Kerry Walker.

What does Emerson have to do with politics?

Everything.

There is so much potential in the word everything.

1

Even I'm Not That Good
Evangeline

"*J*esus Christ, Evangeline!" Darren raises his voice, holding one of the photos in his hand. "Did you fuck him?" he asks harshly. "Did you fuck my father?" he demands, and I blink as if his words are arrows that have hit their target.

"No!"

"Trips out of town, speaking events – now I know why he didn't want my mother to go with him," Darren accuses absently as if he didn't hear me.

"I never saw him again!" I yell to stop him from talking, but that's not the whole truth. "Not after that night." That gets Darren's attention.

"We were talking about Emerson, and Langley…"

"Langley?" Darren's eyes go wide.

"Yes, he was with your father. He wanted to know about my demographic and your father. He was so gracious, and invited me to dinner with his staff. I didn't know the pictures were taken, but nothing happened," I'm out of breath, trying to get it all out at once.

"Bullshit!" Darren roars, scattering the photos so they fly off the desk as if a gust of wind tore through the office.

"He was a senator! They don't invite voters to fucking dinner, Evangeline."

"Your father was interested in what I had to say – about Emerson, about me," I rattle off excuses, but I can feel my chest cave, wondering if my memory of that evening is as reliable as I think. Was I so desperate for someone to pay attention to what I had to say that I didn't see—?

"I'm sure he wanted you there to talk about your demographic." He looks across the desk at me and shakes his head. It makes me feel small and naïve. Maybe I was back then, but now…

"Is it so hard for you to believe that someone would be interested in what I had to say? That someone would be interested in my intellect instead of my body?" I ask, offended, but even I'm beginning to wonder now.

Darren rubs the back of his neck, saying nothing.

"You're an asshole."

"I'm an asshole? You manipulated your way into my life…"

I approach the desk and place my fingers on the dark wood. "You blew up my life so I'd have no choice but to marry you!" I argue, pointing a finger at him as he sits behind the desk, dark eyes staring at me. "You know what's really fucked up, Darren?" He furrows his brows at me. "If you would have just asked me to marry you instead of getting me fired, I probably would have said yes."

He stands, and the chair bangs into the wall, jarring me. There's a flicker of regret before he swipes a hand over his face as if to gain composure.

"I'm an asshole, I admit that." He almost sounds remorseful. "I fucked you over so I could get what I wanted, but I never *once* lied to you." He smacks a pen from the desk and turns away from me.

I stand there like a child who's just been scolded, my cheeks hot, and my heart beating hard against my ribs. Darren may have been underhanded about our union, but I went into it with secrets that I somehow thought would stay buried. How stupid a notion that was.

"And Langley?" His eyes are wide. "You could have told me. You could have warned me you knew him before," Darren fumes.

"Do you want a list of all my clients?" I challenge.

"He's different and you know it!" His voice fills the room. "Did you fuck him, too?" he demands, and my belly drops.

"He didn't get the chance," I admit, and think back to that night as Darren waits for me to continue. "Our date was cut short because of the news…"

"About my parents?" he asks, but he already knows the answer.

He collapses into the chair as if his legs can't hold him up any longer. "I never liked Langley, but God…" He can't finish the sentence after putting the pieces together. Which I'm glad because right now I don't think I could explain this tangled web.

"I'm sure he's the one that had the photos," I accuse. "It makes sense."

"Jesus!" He rubs the back of his neck and stands up again. "If you had told me, I could have done something."

I hug myself as if to keep my insides from spilling out. Heavy shame shivers down my spine. "I… I couldn't," I say honestly.

"What were you doing at that bar?" he demands. "Did you follow me?"

"No!" I exclaim. "I didn't know you were going to be there. I couldn't go home that night, not after finding out about your father. I didn't want to be alone," I admit.

"You could have just left me in that alley." He looks at me with a weary expression.

"I wanted to see…" I whisper, leaving the rest of the sentence hanging, but he grasps my meaning.

"Well, now you know," he says, raising his arms. "I'm nothing like him."

"That's not true."

He doesn't know how very much like his father he is.

"Did you know who I was? In the bar?" he asks, eyes searching mine.

I shake my head no, but that's not true. There was a familiarity when he quoted Emerson. It felt like fate.

I carried a flame for a man who burned bright because he was the only thing bright to hold onto. But he was just a man. He wasn't perfect like I'd made him out to be. He was a husband, a father, a son, and a politician. How could I expect so much from one person I barely knew?

"Yes."

"Fuck," he mutters, running a hand over his mouth while the other is planted on the desk. His head is bowed, the thick, dark wavy hair covering his eyes.

He finally looks back up at me. "Did you fake everything?"

I know what he's asking me, and he wants to know the answer badly, whether he chooses to believe me or not.

I should lie and say that I faked everything, even my orgasms, just to hurt him, to get back at him for putting me in this position, but that's not who I am. In truth, I put myself in this position because I did walk into that alley to see if he was okay, not knowing it would unlock this chain of events.

"No," I say as genuinely as I can.

"Because you're so fucking good at your job," he spits with a resentful tone.

"Because even I'm not that good, Darren." I shake my head understanding how betrayed he must feel.

Only one of the pictures remains on the desk, and the way

his father twirls that single strand of hair between his fingers, and the way I'm looking at him as he does it….

As if he's reading my mind, he asks, "Were you in love with him?"

"I don't know how to answer that," I say honestly.

"It's a simple yes or no, Evangeline," his voice is tortured, coming from somewhere deep within him.

It's not as simple as that. I shake my head, but the words that come out don't match, and how could they? "Yes," I answer, feeling tears burn at the back of my eyes, because for a long time, I thought I was – maybe I still am.

How do you know if you love someone when you've never been loved?

"Do you not see how fucked up this is?"

"Darren, I never meant to hurt you."

He laughs cynically. "You never meant to hurt me?"

He sucks in a breath and then shakes his head while staring down at the desk. "The reason for marrying a prostitute was to avoid drama," he scoffs.

The word prostitute penetrates every vulnerable part of me, but I'm not going to let him know how much he hurt me.

I place my hands on my hips, willing myself not to break. "If you didn't want drama, you'd have to take yourself out of the equation."

He looks annoyed, pressing his lips tightly together.

"Look, this happened in the past," I try to reason with him.

"But it's not in the past, Evangeline. It's sitting here on my *fucking* desk," he growls. "I need to get the fuck out of here."

2

Revisionist History
Darren

"If this is where you go to escape, then I'm seriously worried about you." I turn to look at Alistair, who's wearing a lopsided smile with his hands shoved into the pockets of his gray wool overcoat, looking pleased with himself.

"Do you remember coming here on our seventh-grade field trip?" I ask him, and he walks up the rest of the stone steps to meet me.

"Of course," he replies as we both stare straight ahead at the Lincoln Memorial, a temple-like frame flanked by limestone buttresses, and in the center, Lincoln sits with his left hand clenching the arm of the chair. It's imposing and awe-inspiring, an impressive feat of what man's hands can accomplish when put to the use of good; a symbol that even a country torn apart by war can come together and create something beautiful.

"Did you know that Lincoln is carved from twenty-eight pieces of Georgia marble?" I ask without looking at Alistair, but I already know his attention is on something else.

"I was too busy chasing Poppy McBride around the columns to pay attention to our tour guide," Alistair chuckles lightly.

"Why does that not surprise me?" I smile deeply.

"Because you know me too well," he answers, the hint of a smile on his face, lifting his cold pink cheeks.

"There is a lot of information the tour guides don't tell you about the Lincoln Memorial. For instance, one of the workers must have grabbed the wrong stencil and chiseled an E instead of an F for Future," I explain, pointing towards the North chamber where Lincoln's second inaugural speech is chiseled into the limestone. "They fixed it by filling it in with concrete, but you can still see the flaw if you look hard enough." At this distance it's barely discernible.

"I guess I didn't miss as much as I thought," Alistair muses, propping his foot on the step above as he leans against his thigh.

"I know you don't like history, Alistair," I sigh and look back at Lincoln as he stares past me, perhaps to Washington's memorial across the reflecting pool. "These steps have witnessed history-making moments, such as King's I Have a Dream speech, and yet the tour guides don't tell you that the dedication ceremony was racially segregated." I laugh cynically.

"That's fucked up," Alistair scoffs. "But why are we here, Darren?" he inquires.

"Revisionist history, Alistair," I say, pointing my finger in the air before taking a seat on the step.

It's an unusually lovely day in Washington D.C. with only a few clouds dotting the sky and the sun lighting up the reflecting pool, making it look like tiny diamonds resting on its surface, yet there is a chill in the air, a sign of winter on the horizon when snow will cover the city, bowing the branches of the white oak trees that flank the lawn.

Alistair takes a seat next to me, stretching out his long legs over the marble steps.

"We look back on history and memorialize a great man, but we forget about the flaws; we minimize them. His martyrdom makes it impossible to point them out. It's true that Lincoln had one foot in the 20th century, but the other foot was still planted heavily in the 19th," I lament, "and yet here we sit, on the steps of this memorial that holds the daily pilgrimage of thousands, and we forget about those innate things that made him human."

"We're not really talking about Lincoln, are we?" Alistair asks astutely.

"I didn't get along with my father," I say as a matter of fact. "That's never been in question; a constant since as far back as I can remember, and yet I always looked up to him." I sigh, tilting my head towards Alistair who looks down at his clasped hands resting on his thighs. "But I always thought I knew him. Lately, I'm beginning to question that, to question a lot of things."

"Anything in particular that you didn't know?" he inquires, lifting a brow.

I pull out the envelope and hand it to Alistair. He takes it with questioning eyes and then pulls it open to peer inside at the very thing that makes me question my father's martyrdom. Tough, passionate, a workaholic – everything the Priest said at the pulpit during my parent's memorial – a loyal husband and father – and now I wonder if it was just revisionist history.

"Fuck," he says, closing the envelope as if to keep the secrets from making their way out, and I feel vindicated for my initial reaction. "He was a client?"

I take the envelope and stuff it back into the inside pocket of my jacket.

"No, these were taken four years ago. She was a student,

and my father was giving a speech at her university. She said nothing happened."

"Do you believe her?" The photos are damning without context, but that's the problem with photos – they're up to the interpretation of the viewer.

"Bailey was there when they met and attests to the fact that he drove my father back to his hotel alone."

"That's not what I asked," he questions.

"I wanted to believe her," I admit, peering over at Alistair and pressing my lips tight together. "But it's this part of me," I gesture to the monument, "that needs the facts."

I lean my forearms on my thighs and run my hands through my hair. The cold marble seeps through my jeans causing a chill to run along my spine, goosebumps forming on my arms and legs.

Sometimes we want to know things that we really shouldn't. Seeing the pictures – my father holding a strand of her wheat-colored hair between his fingers – the same hair I'd run my hands through, pressed my face against – was all too much. I can't get the image out of my head; the profile of her full, parted lips, the way her eyes are slightly closed, the shadow of her long lashes cresting the tops of her cheeks. I shake the thought from my mind, the one that has invaded and taken hold of me ever since I saw the photo. It's not that she seems to have my father captivated, but that she is looking at him in a way that she would never look at me.

Am I so fucked up that I'm jealous of a dead man?

"Who gave those to you?" Alistair's question breaks through my thoughts, and I raise an eyebrow at him. "Rausch?" He gives a dark laugh.

"I know he's pissed that you circumvented the will, but now that it's done, what does it matter to him?"

"Other than to gloat that he was right about marrying her?" I scoff. "I'm not worried about that." I shake my head. "It's who he got the photos from that I'm worried about."

"If the press had gotten ahold of them..." Alistair doesn't finish his sentence, but he doesn't have to. This would be a huge scandal, whether it was an innocent interaction or not. Politics runs on perception, not to mention the media storm that would descend on Evangeline.

Even though I'm angry, I wouldn't wish that upon her or the destruction of my parents' reputation.

"Someone's had these for four years, Alistair," I point out, my voice sounding grave with the weight of it. "I have a feeling it was Langley."

"But what would he have to gain from that?" Alistair asks. "Rumor around Washington was that he was going to be your father's first pick as a running mate."

Something my father taught me – Presidential elections aren't won in the final hour. Presidents are made decades before they even run.

"Do you have any idea how my life would have been if my father ran for President?"

Alistair offers me a small smile.

"I'm a selfish prick, I already know this."

"Maybe you and Lincoln have something in common."

I laugh at the absurdity.

"You're both human."

Alistair stands, as do I. "How did you even know I was here?"

He chuckles, giving me a sideways smile. "I've been trying to get hold of you so I went to the house. I thought you'd taken off to Atlantic City or somewhere fun without me," he continues. "I would have been pissed, because yes, I have a job, but that doesn't mean I'm dead in the water," Alistair continues, sounding offended.

"Does your boss hold this same sentiment?"

Alistair's smile turns into that of a Cheshire Cat, and I shake my head.

"Jesus, are you fucking your boss?"

"Not yet," he raises a conspiratorial eyebrow. "But I have her wrapped around my finger."

I cross my arms over my chest and stare at him disbelievingly.

"Okay, mostly," Alistair acquiesced with a shrug.

I laugh. "Well, in that case, I would never dream of leaving you behind."

"What did she say when you went to the house?" I ask, trying to sound casual.

"She told me to go fuck myself," he laughs.

I cough into my fist to keep a laugh from escaping. *Fuck.* I shake my head thinking about what her expression might have been as she slammed the door in his face.

"Then how did you know I was here?"

"I told you before, we've known each other for a long time, Dare. As much as you may think you're nothing like your father, he loved this shit too." Alistair motions around the National Mall. "And apparently, so do you." He presses a finger to my chest.

"You went to *The Tombs* first, didn't you?" I accuse.

"And just about every fucking memorial in the Mall," he admits with exaggeration. "My feet are killing me," he complains, looking down at his shiny dress shoes.

"Now that I believe," I chuckle.

Alistair puts his arm around my shoulders and we walk down the steps of the monument. "Why were you looking for me anyway?"

"I got my series seven," Alistair boasts, barely containing his excitement.

"Congratulations." I know Alistair wouldn't comb all over Washington just to tell me that, so I wait for the bomb to drop.

"Which means I'm a qualified trader, my friend." He raises his eyebrows and now I know what he wants.

"No. Absolutely not." I shake my head. "I am not investing my money with you."

"Come on, Dare," he begs. "I need to show the firm I'm bringing in money."

"Go solicit some unsuspecting friend of your father," I offer.

"You don't think I tried that?" He lowers his arms to his sides, looking defeated.

"Do not give me the puppy dog look. It might work on women who don't know you, but it's not going to work on me."

"For one, I do not have to beg women to sleep with me, and two," he pauses, "well, I don't have a two, but Darren…" he calls behind me as I turn to escape. "Dammit, don't walk away from me."

Feeling my phone vibrate in my pocket, I hold my hand up for Alistair to stop as I take a call. He rolls his eyes.

"Sir, I've been notified that the jet is ready for flight," Bailey explains on the other end.

"What are you talking about?"

"The crew called me to find out if you would be joining."

On occasion my father would lend the plane to a friend or colleague, but I can't imagine anyone would call in such a favor now. The thought of it upsets me even more so than if the crew had made a mix-up.

"Bailey, I don't know what you're talking about." I start to get agitated.

"I don't think Evangeline knew that the flight crew would alert anyone."

Evangeline?

Fuck!

"What's going on?" Alistair asks, the creases of concern fanning his eyes.

"Evangeline's leaving, and she's taking my fucking plane." My heart races and the sudden change makes me feel dizzy. Never did I think she would actually leave – especially when she knows what's at stake.

"Leaving?" he asks, tilting his head in confusion. "Does she know she's not getting any money unless she stays the whole year?"

"She knows damn well!" I yell, pacing along the steps. But if I thought Evangeline cared about the money, I'd have bought her a closet full of designer gowns, fur coats, or whatever the *fuck* she wanted.

She'd rather leave penniless then stay with me.

I press the phone to my ear and ask to be patched into the pilot.

"What's the destination?" I ask before the pilot can utter a word.

"Sorry, Mr. Walker?"

"Where the *fuck* is my wife going?" I fume.

"Las Vegas, sir," the captain confirms. "Do you want me to cancel the flight?"

I stare at the dirty wet pavement while I contemplate his question. When I look at Alistair, he's staring back at me bewildered.

I have been a fuckup all my life – on purpose – not because I didn't know any better. I have done stupid, selfish things because I thought I had to in order to get what I wanted. She said she would have married me if I had just asked her. Maybe I can leave the choice up to her.

"No."

3
The Things I've Done
Evangeline

I drag my luggage into the kitchen and stop when I see Lottie, but it's too late to back out because she's already noticed me.

"Evangeline!" Lottie smiles, peeking around the refrigerator door, her eyes stopping on my luggage. She finishes placing a carton of milk on the shelf and knocks the door shut with her hip.

"Good morning." I glance towards the front door, willing my rideshare to hurry up and get here.

"Would you like some breakfast? I made scones," she offers in a cheerful tone while ignoring my luggage, at least for now.

I shake my head. "I don't have time."

I don't think I could stomach anything right now anyway.

"Well, surely you have time for a cup of coffee." She doesn't take no for an answer easily, and since my rideshare hasn't arrived yet, I reluctantly take the seat opposite her at the kitchen island.

"Are you going on a trip?" she inquires casually while grabbing a cup from the nearby cupboard.

"Not exactly," I manage to say. "Have you seen Darren?" I ask not so subtly. He left and hasn't come back, which is probably a good thing right now.

"Darren can be difficult," she replies, sliding the cup of coffee towards me, and I'm grateful to have something solid to hold onto. "But he usually comes around."

"Difficult, yes," I nod. "Coming around? Not so sure about that."

"I know it's none of my business," she admits, resting her arms on the island, "but when Will and I got married, I had this silly notion that it would always be like our honeymoon." She offers a small smile. "We had to learn how to be with one another in the real world." She pushes away from the island and finishes putting away the groceries.

"I don't think this is the same situation," I admit, feeling like a fraud – especially with Lottie.

"You're right, it's not. You and Darren got married under very different circumstances," she offers, making me wonder what she knows. "Losing his parents has been difficult for him. I know he pretends that it doesn't bother him, but believe me, it does."

"Some things don't get a pass in the name of tragedy. At some point, you have to grow up," I state, knowing it sounds harsh, but I'm not inclined to make excuses for Darren – especially when I know exactly how he feels about me.

"I know you think I'm making excuses for him. Lord knows Darren can push your limits, but everyone deserves a little grace."

Lottie has a knack for reading people's minds.

"I think you're a better woman than me," I sigh.

"That's not true."

"You don't know me or the things I've done." I doubt Lottie has ever had to make the choices I've had to make.

"We've all done things we're not proud of. Doesn't make you a bad person. It just makes you a person who's had to make tough choices." She reaches out to take my hand, but I pull away. I'm feeling very vulnerable right now, and if I let her touch me, she'll be able to extracts truths I'm not ready to let go of.

Lottie seems to take my silence as a way of agreement, but I stare at the entryway wishing my car would arrive.

"I'm sure he'll be back soon," she tries to reassure me. "You can always work things out."

"That's not what I'm worried about. Even when he does come back, then what?"

"You argue until one of you gives in," she explains. "Then you go upstairs and make love until you forget about what it is you were arguing about in the first place," she states matter-of-factly.

If I had taken a sip of coffee, I might have spit it out all of over the island. Lottie always seems to surprise me.

"I only wish it were that easy," I counter.

The doorbell rings and I slide off the chair. Before I reach my luggage, Lottie stops me by placing a gentle hand on my arm.

"Don't give up on him." I know she cares for Darren deeply, it's evident in the worried expression on her face, but this isn't up to me.

"I have to go." I hesitate for a moment before I give her a brief hug and head for the door.

I shouldn't be emotional over saying goodbye to Lottie, but in the short time I've been here, she's been more of a mother than I've had in a very long time.

It's a short ride to the airport. As we cross the Potomac, I can't help but think of the first time I crossed it, seeing the city I had fantasized about for so long. My hands are shaking, and to stop them, I hold my purse tighter.

I never belonged here, and I was kidding myself if I ever

thought I did. I need the money, but it's not worth it. I'll figure something out – I always do.

Just to piss him off, I chartered Darren's private plane. After everything he's done, I figure I deserved at least a nice ride back home.

The driver holds out my luggage and whistles at the plane sitting on the tarmac. "Sure must be nice to have a private jet," he says.

"I'm sure it is, but it's not mine." I hand him what little cash I have on me as the stewardess descends the stairs.

She takes my luggage with a smile. "Welcome aboard, Mrs. Walker."

She says the name so effortlessly... but I'm nothing but a fraud, playing pretend wife in a mansion, boarding a private jet that isn't mine.

Now that I'm on the plane, I'm not so sure it was a good idea.

On the seat is a book. *A Moveable Feast* by Ernest Hemingway, and a small laugh escapes me. "Asshole," I whisper as I settle in and flip through the pages.

"I'll let you know when we're ready for takeoff," the stewardess says and then disappears.

I hold the book to my nose inhaling the worn pages, and thinking about how many times I've read it. I may not have understood poetry when I was in college, but Hemingway had an immersive way of telling a story that made me feel a part of it; so much so that I already felt like I had been to Paris.

First editions of this book aren't worth an exorbitant amount, and I imagine Darren would have a snarky comment about how Hemingway is undervalued.

It was incredibly sweet of Darren to remember our conversation and get it for me, but that was before. Now, holding it in my hands, I'm not sure what to make of it or how I should feel. The Emerson portrait, the book… everything… it doesn't matter now.

My phone vibrates in my back pocket, and when I look at the caller my stomach tightens.

"Is everything okay with Mimi?" I ask, my pulse quickening.

"She's having a good day today, and she was asking for you," her nurse, Maria, explains immediately, making me feel better.

I used to speak to Mimi every Sunday morning and she'd tell me about her week, like what dessert she had with dinner, and what they watched for movie night. In the last year, she's started to forget who I am. When she puts Mimi on the phone for me, I have to fight back the rush of emotions at hearing her voice.

"Evan, are you taking care of yourself?" she asks sweetly.

"Yes, Mimi."

"You're not overdoing it at the paper, are you? You work too hard."

I hold the phone tight to my ear. "I'm not overdoing it."

"When am I going to get to read something of yours in the paper?" she asks, her voice excited and proud.

I swallow hard before I say, "Hopefully soon. Journalism is very competitive."

I hate lying to her, but most of the time she doesn't remember what I told her, and if it makes her happy to think that I graduated and am now working at a paper, then I'll play along. If she knew what I did to pay for her care she'd never forgive me. Not that she'd judge me harshly, but to know that I'd given up my dreams would destroy her.

"You tell them I said to run your articles," she demands with all seriousness, "or I'll come down there and give them a whack with my cane."

She's been confined to a wheelchair for the last couple of years and hasn't used a cane since then, but I laugh anyway, picturing her poking someone in order to get them to print my fictional article.

"You can't go around threatening people, Mimi."

"Well, why not?"

I giggle. "Because it's not polite."

"Oh pfffft," she says.

I always loved her feistiness.

"I've missed you so much," I say with a shaky voice.

"Well, honey, I've been right here," she says.

"I know." I cover the phone speaker so she doesn't hear me fighting to keep the tears at bay. It's not just her, but this whole situation I've managed to get myself into.

"Oh, honey, Maria wants to talk to you before we hang up. Dirty Dancing is playing tonight and I don't want to miss the Swayze."

I blurt out, "I love you," but she's already handed the phone to Maria.

"She sounded good today."

"She seems to be responding to the new medication Dr. Rakesh has her on, but it's too soon to tell if it will be consistent. Um, Evangeline, Medicare isn't going to be covering the medication anymore."

"Why? If it seems to be helping, isn't that a good thing? You'd think Medicare would want to prevent having to cover costly treatments if she wasn't *on* the medication," I bark into the phone knowing it's not Maria's fault, but I have no one else to take my frustration out on.

Dealing with insurance companies and doctors over the years has left me with little patience.

"Honey, the one thing I've learned after all these years dealing with insurance companies is that they'll do anything to avoid having to pay for something."

It's the same experience I've had trying to get Mimi's treatments paid for with no results.

"How much is the prescription?" I have a sinking feeling that it's not cheap.

"I'll have to look it up to be sure, but we're talking at least four figures a month."

It feels like the air has been pushed out of my lungs, and I desperately fight to keep the tears at bay, but I'm tired. I'm tired of swimming against the current. This just might be the last straw that sinks me.

"What do you want me to do?" Maria inquires cautiously.

I lean over my lap just trying to catch my breath; my lungs feel like they're caving in on me.

"Evan?" Maria prods.

I manage to sit up and when I look around the plane, I can't help but notice the opulence – from the elegant lighting, the bar, the TVs, and the leather seats. It looks like you could be in someone's living room instead of a plane.

"Have Dr. Rakesh fill the prescription."

"Your grandmother is so lucky to have you."

"Thank you, Maria," I work to keep my voice even. "I'll talk to you later, I have to go."

I hang up the phone quickly before she can say anything else and hold my head in my hands. The book sits in my lap and I stare at the cover, a picture of the Seine in Paris that blurs with each drop of my tears.

"We're almost ready to taxi, just waiting for clearance," the stewardess interrupts my thoughts.

I quickly wipe the tears from my eyes and spring from my seat. "I can't leave," I say panicked, hoping it's not too late to get off.

"I'm sorry, ma'am?" she asks, confused.

"I have to go." I leave the book on the seat in a rush as I make my way to the door. "I'm so sorry."

4
Fucking Hemingway
Darren

*T*ake the stairs two at a time, and when I get to the top, I hear a slosh of water come from the guest bedroom. She didn't leave but she was going to, and the thought has me all tied up in knots.

Standing in the doorway, I take a deep breath and peer inside, noticing how it *looks* like a guest room – nothing personal of Evangeline's, not even a scented candle or a book of poetry on the nightstand to show that she lives here.

My faded Georgetown t-shirt lays rumpled on the bed as if she'd slept in it. I bring it to my nose and it smells like her – vanilla and cherry blossoms – no sign of my expensive cologne. The thought of her sleeping in my shirt does things to me... wicked things.

The ensuite door is cracked open enough to see the steam on the mirror. I push it open, noticing her hair pulled into a bun with a few wet strands clinging to the side of her neck as she rests her head on the edge. Bubbles annoyingly obscure everything aside from a kneecap that crests the surface. I've never been so mesmerized by such a simple sliver of exposed skin before in my life, but when it dips under the bubbles, I find myself desperately disappointed.

All the anger I had felt before slowly ebbs away – not completely, but enough for me to enter the room. She doesn't seem shocked by my presence. She just looks at me with an annoyed expression that I find tempting. It's the way her eyes narrow into an almond shape and her lips press together to form an alluring pout that pulls out the dark desire from deep within me. Even the anger and the hurt that's still under the surface does little to suffocate the need for her.

I shouldn't want her.

But I do.

I want her in a way that defies reason when I should hate her – when the pain inside of me turns into a ball of jealous hate for any man that has touched her – even if that man was my father.

"Did Alistair bail you out, or was he in there with you?" she muses sarcastically, and pushes her hand through the bubbles to grip the edge.

I cross my hands over my chest with my feet apart and stare down at her, the bubbles now barely covering her breasts. My eyes track the movement of her foot as she lifts it out of the water and places it on the edge near the faucet.

"Fortunately, I wasn't in jail, but so nice of you to care, *wife*."

"No one said anything about caring." She turns away, and I can't help but smile at the defiant expression on her face.

"Not sure I believe that, but…"

She whips her head around. "I don't care what you believe, but since we're on the subject, Darren, you're a grown man or so you claim to be, and you can do whatever you want, but when it involves my integrity…"

"Your integrity?"

"Yes, my integrity," she sneers, "because when I tell you

something, it's the truth. I have no reason to lie, and you just leave like a child who didn't get his way," she finishes.

"Look who's talking. I know all about the jet. Nice, by the way. Did you think they wouldn't alert me?"

Her face falls.

"You're still here."

"Yes, Darren. I'm still here."

"Why is that, if I'm such an asshole?"

"You're very good at it, too."

She doesn't answer the damn question, and I rub my chin in frustration.

"Mechanical difficulties?" I inquire, lifting an eyebrow.

"No."

"Was it the book?" I give I her a cocky grin. It's not exactly the way I wanted her to find it, but it's been eating me up inside ever since I found out she chartered the plane.

She laughs. Correction, it's more like a scoff. "Be careful, Darren, or your ego will cause your head to explode."

Fucking Hemingway.

I scratch my head. "Forgive me for being nice."

"You could teach a class in passive aggressive behavior, you know that?" she accuses.

"You can't even begin to understand what I'm going through!" I snap.

"Your parents died unexpectedly, but at a certain point, that excuse doesn't work anymore, and then you're just a plain asshole." Her animated gestures cause the water to slosh over the edge of the tub, creating a pool at my feet.

"You hide fucking information from me and *I'm* the asshole?" I ask, getting heated.

"So now you want to talk? Okay, Darren." She sits up in the tub, her knees poking through the bubbles. "And what if I *had* told you, would that have changed anything? Would you still have *coerced* me into marrying you?" she asks, and I watch droplets of water fall down her long neck.

"I don't know, but at least I'd have made an informed decision." I know damn well I would have still wanted her.

"Don't give me your judgmental look, because what I did with *my* life before you is my business!" she fumes, flinging soapy water at me.

"Hey!" I look down at my jeans, now wet with bubbles. "Don't act like you're innocent because I know what you think of me," I accuse, but I can't help noticing how the bubbles seem to be dissipating from the tub, allowing me to see the rosebud of her nipples peeking out through the water.

"And what do I think of you, Darren?" she asks, splashing more of the water and bubbles at me. "That you're a spoiled brat who doesn't know what it's like to have to work for everything you have?"

I provoke her more by adding, "Not true," I lift my eyebrows. "I clerked for Judge Hopkins, but then Alistair had to go and defile his daughter and got me fired."

"You're disgusting," she splashes more water at me. My pants are now soaked and my shirt is plastered to my chest. "You and Alistair deserve each other. You should have married him."

Only a few bubbles are left, leaving the water semitransparent, and my stomach tightens. My fingers twitch and I shove them in my pockets. Giving in would let her know how much she affects me, and I've already given her too much ammunition.

"Alistair would have asked for ten million. You were a bargain."

That rewards me with a splash of water to my face. "Jesus, Evan! At this rate I should just join you in the bathtub," I say, while shaking the wet hair from my face.

I blink back the water and adjust my vision, locking eyes with her. The water ripples around her pert nipples which are floating above the line; a dusky pink, the color of one of the roses in the garden. She's playing with fire when she relaxes her legs, letting her thighs fall open and giving me a better view of her pussy which is just begging for me to pull back the layers and sink my tongue inside. A deep groan works its way up my throat, and I pull at the collar of my shirt. The air is thick and humid, and I can feel the hairs at the back of my neck curl.

Despite everything, knowing that she omitted certain important information, and the fact that she may still be in love with my father, I still feel I made the right decision in marrying her. No debutant would spread her legs like this, giving me a view of her bare cunt, and by the look on her face, love it.

She knows I'm staring and I couldn't pull my eyes away even if a train ran right through the middle of the bathroom. She surprises me by throwing the soapy sponge in my face. Right in my fucking eyes.

"Shit!" I blindly feel around and find a towel to wipe my eyes.

She stands, wraps a towel around herself, and leaves.

"You didn't tell me why you didn't leave!" I call after her.

"Five million dollars!" she says.

5

It's A Long List
Evangeline

J pull the door open to the cafe and see a familiar silver-haired, elegant woman at the counter. I thought taking a walk through the park would put some distance between me and Darren, but running into Audrina squashes that.

"Evangeline," she beams.

I let go of the door handle and take my place in line.

"Audrina Ellwood." She holds her slender hand out to introduce herself to me again, as if I could forget meeting her. The mental image that Darren put in my head of her wearing a dominatrix outfit whipping donations out of D.C.'s upper crust almost makes me laugh.

Goddammit, Darren.

"So nice to see you again." I extend my hand to take hers. "Sorry it's cold, I was just out for a walk," I attempt to explain my disheveled appearance. My hair has started to come undone from my ponytail and my jacket and sweatpants don't compare to Audrina's elegant red cashmere coat and designer heels.

"Ah, well, the only refreshing walk I get is rushing across Pennsylvania avenue without getting run over I'm afraid," she teases.

The line moves up. "Excuse me," I say and order a flat white, digging into my jacket pocket to pay and then notice Audrina waiting for me by the pick-up counter.

"I'm so glad I ran into you."

I'm beginning to doubt it was a coincidence.

"I wanted to talk to you about the foundation."

I can feel my cheeks heat at the thought of what happened at the charity event, and I can only imagine what she thinks of me. "I'm sorry about ruining the event," I apologize.

"Oh please, you didn't ruin anything," she brushes me off.

"I don't know what got into Darren, but he's very sorry for causing a scene," I make an excuse – more for my sake than for Darren's.

"I think the evening was a bit more emotional for him then he anticipated. In fact, I probably shouldn't have pushed him into making a speech so soon after Merrill," she pauses, taking a breath.

"Anyway, I wanted to ask what role you'd like in the foundation. I mean, I understand you wouldn't want to take on everything right away, but at least get your feet wet," she starts to explain, but before she can finish, the barista calls out her order to be picked up.

"Oh, I wasn't planning on…" But what am I going to tell her, that my marriage is an arrangement?

"But you must," her voice is shrill. "You're a Walker. Certainly Darren explained things?"

"Explained what things?" I ask, confused.

"Oh, I thought he would have…" she pauses, shaking her head. "I'm sure he's been busy. He has my number. Call me and we can go over everything."

I barely have time to register anything before she says her

goodbyes, a gust of wind whipping through the café as the door slowly closes in her wake.

"Flat white!" the barista calls out, and I take my drink to one of the empty tables by the window.

Someone left an old copy of *The Post*, and I notice the photo on the front of Kerry and Merrill's memorial at the National Cathedral. I flip through the pages to get to the rest of the article and see a picture of Darren and me entering the church. I'm pleasantly surprised that there isn't a mention of *when* we married, just a caption listing our names: Darren and Evangeline Walker. I can't help but notice our hands clasped together as we take the stairs to the entrance of the church.

My phone vibrates against my thigh.

"Hi, honey, how ya doing?" Cleo's clear voice on the other end brings a smile to my face.

"I'm okay," I sigh, folding the paper and pushing it to the side.

"Uh oh, that doesn't sound good. Is Darren freaky? Let me guess, he has a playroom – likes pain – does he make you dress up in a maid's outfit?" Cleo teases, and I can't help but laugh.

"No, but I did have to dress up like Jessica Rabbit and wear a mask, does that count?" I give a light laugh.

"Ooh, kinky," Cleo laughs undeterred.

"Not quite, it was for a charity event," I explain.

"You don't sound happy," she notices.

I can hear the creak of the couch as she shifts her weight, most likely curling up like a cat. I've never felt more homesick than I do now, and that's probably why I haven't called her.

"If I was getting five million dollars to marry a man as young and handsome as Darren Walker, I would dress up like Jessica Rabbit every day," she whistles.

I chuckle into the phone. "Money isn't everything," I remind her.

"I'm covering my ears and pretending I didn't hear that," she jokes.

"It's just very different then I thought it would be," I admit.

"What's different?"

I want to say that I didn't expect to have all these emotions swirling around inside me, but that would open me up to Cleo's scrutiny. She doesn't know that I live in the house of a man that I pined over for four years. I can barely admit it to myself.

Instead, I say, "I didn't think I would be roped into the board of a charity foundation." An expectation that Darren didn't mention anything about to me. Was I really expected to take something on like that with legitimate wives of politicians, doctors, and well-to-dos? Not to mention, I have no experience working on a charity. I can't help but wonder if Darren didn't say anything to me on purpose.

"Is that really all?" Cleo challenges. "Because working on a charity sounds like a good thing. How else are you going to spend your time – besides shopping?"

Her question strikes me like an arrow, because I don't have an answer. I didn't think that far ahead. I'd spent so much time just keeping my head above water that I never had a chance to think about the future. Now, I have what seems like an endless amount of time.

"I don't know. I'll have to think about it," I sigh. "Tell me, what have you been up to?" I ask to take the heat off myself, and mostly so that I can hear her voice some more.

My walk hadn't cleared my mind. It only served to make it more cloudy. When I get back to the house I head straight for the gym. I've only used it a handful of times, preferring to get in a run outside, but the weather has turned into the cool, wet fall I had always imagined as a kid who grew up in the desert. I wasn't used to different seasons and the way the weather can change so drastically throughout the day. I find myself enjoying the rain, and the way the trees change colors and lose their leaves as if shedding away the old to make way for the new.

As I finish my set, Darren stops abruptly in the doorway.

The silence in the gym is tangible. Our eyes lock in the mirror. I once thought the house was too big for only two people, but now it feels suffocatingly small. He breaks the stare by sitting down on the weight bench behind me. His perpetually messy brown locks fall into his eyes as he leans down to set his water bottle on the floor. There's a two-day old shadow of hair along his jaw. He's wearing a navy Hoyas t-shirt that stretches across his chest, annoyingly too small, showing the definition of his youthful physique.

I watch as he lays down on the bench, sliding under the barbell. Hesitating for a moment, he looks in my direction, catching me watching. The grin on his face causes me to look away. "I would ask you to spot me, but after you almost took my eye out, I'm not sure if you'd try to suffocate me, too."

"Probably a good call." I set the bar back on the rack and grab my water bottle.

"You could have caused permanent damage to my eye," Darren grunts, taking a drink from his sports bottle.

"Don't be dramatic." I sit on the mat, wiping sweat from my forehead.

Darren pulls his shirt off, making a show of it, and lays back down on the bench positioning his hands on the barbell. Now that the extra weight is off, he lifts it easily from the rack, his stomach muscles contracting, giving him that deep V cut that runs under the waistband of his sweatpants. I wish I was immune to how good-looking he is, especially because I'm still pissed at him, but I'm not.

Snapping out of it, I throw the towel on the floor beside me and say, "You know you can't just barge in on me whenever you want."

"Sorry, I thought since I'd already tasted your cunt, modesty was the last thing to worry about."

His words cause me to swallow hard, but his ambivalence irritates me.

"That's not the point, especially since you don't even sleep in there with me."

Parting my legs into a V, I lean forward into a deep stretch. My ponytail falls forward as I rest my forearms on the mat when I see Darren's gym shoes planted in front of me. I tip my head, my eyes traveling up his legs to his stomach where his sweatpants sit tantalizingly low on his hips – maybe a bit too low. Maybe even on purpose.

"I wasn't aware that you wanted me in your bed." He lifts an eyebrow, his deep voice full of innuendo.

"I don't."

He makes a disbelieving noise, then grabs one of the free weights. I watch the veins travel up his forearm as if waking from slumber.

He's looking at me with an amused expression, the corners of his lips pulling into a smug smile that makes me want to smack him.

"Plotting how you can get maximum force to kick me in the balls, or do you just like the view?" he muses smugly, continuing to curl the weight, making sure to flex his muscle with exaggeration.

It's a nice view, I have to give him that. My expression turns to a scowl. "Hmm, tempting," I affirm. "You're in my personal space." I motion to the area around me and realizing that I sound childish, but I don't care.

"Your long-ass legs are taking up the whole floor." He scowls down at me, but his eyes still hold the hint of mischief while he skims over my bare legs, to the sliver of bare skin at my stomach, until finally reaching my face. I bend my knees and stand up, facing him.

"Since when do you work out anyway?" I inquire. "Other than using your forearm to lift a glass of whiskey."

"For your information, I played Lacrosse in college."

I scoff, turning on the treadmill, determined to drown him out with the sound of the belt running.

"Are you going to enlighten me on what today's attitude's for?" Darren probes, causing me to pull a face.

My attitude stems from when he got me fired, coerced me into marrying him, and then accused me of fucking his father, but that argument was becoming stale.

"It's a long list, Darren," I glower, while continuing to run, wishing I hadn't forgotten my headphones, because then I could tune him out. "But today's attitude is because you volunteered me for Audrina's charity and didn't discuss it with me first."

"It's my *mother's* charity," he corrects with a darkened expression.

I feel heat flood my face because I know Darren's mother is a sensitive subject, and I've always tried to be respectful about that.

"Besides, I thought you liked charity work, what with the homeless and all."

Usually while running I can tune everything out, train my mind to focus on one single point to push through the ache in my lungs. That one single point right now is Darren's abs. He's such a selfish, annoying man.

Shaking those dangerous thoughts from my head, I snap, "You should have warned me Audrina was going to ambush me at the cafe this morning."

"What makes you think I knew?"

"The cafe is not exactly the kind of place someone like Audrina would hang out," I offer.

"You're been here, what, a month, and you already have everyone pegged?" he challenges.

"Why does that surprise you? Because I'm not a college graduate?"

He crosses his arms and his soft hazel eyes settle on me, and I let out a jagged breath.

"I should have known Audrina would track you down," Darren lets out a frustrated sigh. "She can be resourceful."

"What the fuck is wrong with you people?" I ask angrily, meeting Darren's startled gaze.

"You people?"

"It's been nothing but games since I met you."

I step down from the treadmill to face him.

"You don't get it, Darren."

We stand toe to toe.

"You brought me here. You put me in a situation where I couldn't…" I falter, looking into his eyes that soften with shades of worry. "A situation I wasn't prepared to handle."

Darren steps closer. "If I had known about your history…"

"You mean the one where I'm a prostitute?"

"The one where you knew my father." He looks down at me, his jaw sharp and his brow glistening with sweat. "And Langley," he says through gritted teeth.

I shake my head. "Half my client list was in attendance at that charity event."

"Don't say things like that." His eyes flare with annoyance.

I take a dangerous step forward.

"I've got news for you, Darren Walker." I look up at him through my lashes and I can feel his breath on my lips, our closeness causing my skin to pebble with goosebumps. "I'm not a virgin."

His lips press into a tight line, and I watch his Adam's apple bob as he swallows hard.

He lifts his hand as if to touch my face, but I don't give

him the chance and turn away to grab my bottle of water, nearly emptying the whole thing.

Darren runs a hand through his hair instead. "Jesus Christ, Evan. I punched a U.S. senator for you!" He raises his voice, but it's not an angry voice or even one laced with regret.

The room becomes quiet enough to hear the rain hit against the windowpane.

"You punched a U.S. Senator for me," I say quietly.

Darren reacts to my grateful and soft tone by returning the same. "I don't like being blindsided."

"Then why didn't you tell me about Audrina?" I can't keep the hurt from my tone. "Because I'm not a Walker, not really? Or is it because you didn't want someone like me staining your mother's charity?"

His brows furrow, causing deep lines in his forehead. "Is that how you think I see you?"

"You made that pretty clear the other day."

"I was angry, and I shouldn't have said those things," he offers, which I appreciate.

"What was it about him?" he suddenly asks, and I can tell what it takes for him to be so vulnerable.

"Darren, when I met him, I wasn't in a good place. I was drowning in work and school. Everything felt bleak, and then I listened to your father's lecture. He gave me something that I hadn't had in a long time." I pause, feeling the weight of his stare and my insecurities claw at my insides. "He inspired me, and I held onto that, especially when I really needed something to cut through the darkness."

A look of understanding passes over his face, but he remains silent.

"I'm sure if Audrina knew the truth, she wouldn't want to have anything to do with me," I shrug, acting as if it doesn't bother me, but it sits heavy in my stomach.

"You're probably right, but I don't care what Audrina

thinks. You're my wife, and if you wanted to run the whole fucking foundation she has no say in it!"

"Then why didn't you tell me?"

"I never got the chance," he stops short, scratching the back of his head, and even though he doesn't finish the sentence, I know it was because of the photos. "She thought I was keeping you all to myself," he admits with a heavy sigh.

"And were you?" I already know the answer, but I like pushing him.

"You know I do," he admits darkly. "You probably won't believe this, but if you knew my mother, I think she would have been happy to see you take over her charity, if that's what you wanted."

"That's hard to believe."

"She would have seen the same thing in you that she saw in my father," he admits. "She would see what I see."

I turn away from Darren, unable to be under the heavy weight of his stare a moment longer.

As angry as I am, I have to admit that hanging around this house, doing nothing for the next year, doesn't sound fun. My shoulders loosen and I contemplate whether I really want to get in deeper with these people.

When I stare out the window, the sky is still full of clouds, and droplets of rain streak down the glass pane obscuring the view. It's not just the rain but how bare the trees are that reminds me the holidays are almost here, and I can feel my chest tighten at the thought.

It's the ache that makes the decision for me.

"I'll call Audrina tomorrow," I say quietly while I throw my towel into the bin by the door.

"You don't have to."

"I know."

Darren digs into the pocket of his sweatpants, a curious expression on his face as he presses the phone to his ear.

"Alistair, this better be important because…" he starts to

say and then his eyes widen. "You're where?" he asks with amusement. "Well," he sits down on the bench, barely containing his laughter. "I know it's not funny."

He looks over at me, the green flecks in his eyes twinkling with obvious amusement. It's not often he laughs like this, so uninhibited and genuine.

"Just answer me this," he pauses, "did they have to call in a female officer to pat you down?"

6

Don't Be Dramatic
Darren

"Just get me out of here," Alistair growls as he pushes past me, his ankle giving out, and he almost topples over in his heels. There's a loud squeak as Evangeline tries to contain her laughter by pressing a fist to her mouth, but she's not doing a good job of it.

"When you said you were at a police station, you didn't mention it was the *park* police," I accuse.

"Did I need to?" Alistair places his hands on his hips which only makes me laugh harder. "Every police station is the same."

"I disagree."

"Did you have to bring her?" He points to Evangeline, who is doubled over laughing.

"She's my wife," I remind him, amused. "And besides—" I pause, meeting her eyes. "I owed her."

"Jesus Christ. Where's your car parked?" Alistair looks around.

"Car?" I scoff, acting confused. "I'm not parking my BMW in this neighborhood. We took the subway."

47

"Tell me you're joking, because I'm not riding the subway in a dress." Alistair looks alarmed and I almost feel bad for teasing him, but he just makes it so fun. "Call Bailey," he demands.

"Darren," Evangeline warns between giggles.

"I'm joking, the car is in the lot down the street," I tell him.

Momentarily he looks relieved, but then stares down the block with a forlorn expression. Turning back to me, he says, "Did you have to park so far away? My feet are killing me in these heels." He points down to the pair of diamond studded stilettos. I didn't even know they made women's shoes that big.

"Just take them off!"

Alistair stares at me with incredulity. "Do you know what excrements are on this sidewalk?" He pulls a disgusted face. "I could get typhoid."

"I'm no doctor, but I believe typhoid was eradicated back in nineteen forty-five."

"What are you, a doctor?"

"Here, let me help you," Evangeline interjects, holding out an arm to steady him as we start to walk down the sidewalk.

The click of Alistair's heels causes another bout of laughter to bubble up inside me, and I can see the shake of Evangeline's shoulders ahead of me. Alistair's hand is clutched onto her bicep as if his life depends on it and it very well may as he walks unsteadily. I wonder how he got around all night in those.

"Explain to me again what the purpose of this is?" I catch up to them and gesture to his outfit: an evening dress, complete with pearls.

Alistair takes a moment as if he's deciding whether he wants to say something in front of Evangeline or not. He looks down at her arm as she holds onto him, the only thing keeping him upright at the moment, and then sighs.

"As you know, I got my series seven," Alistair starts, as if he's giving a monologue in a Shakespearean play, and I gesture for him to get to the point. "There was this party with the guys at work," he explains, losing his balance as his heel catches in one of the sidewalk cracks. "Shit!" he calls out.

Evangeline giggles while trying to hold him up, and Alistair glares at her. "You try walking in these things," he pouts.

Evangeline presses her lips together.

"Anyway…" I try to get him to finish the story.

"You remember the frat parties?" he asks, and I groan, remembering exactly what he's referring to.

"Like a Halloween party?" Evangeline inquires, curiously.

"Not exactly," I grumble.

"More like a theme party," Alistair explains. "Ya know, like nineties boy bands, seventies, stuff like that. One of them was where the guys dressed up in women's clothes, and the girls dressed up like men."

"Nineties boy bands?" Evangeline asks with a raised eyebrow, and when she turns towards me, it almost looks like she's picturing me as Donnie Wahlberg – as if.

"There is no photographic evidence of this in case you were wondering if you could use it against me."

"Hmm, I doubt that, but if it makes you feel safer," she leaves the sentence hanging, giving me a mischievous smirk and making me want to take a bite of those sexy, pouty lips.

Oblivious to my thoughts, Alistair continues. "I was told by my friends at work that everyone was dressing up, and then I get to the party and I'm the only one." Alistair lifts his arms in the air in exaggeration, nearly toppling over again.

"Can you *really* call them friends at this point?" I ask.

"Don't be jealous, Darren," Alistair places a hand on my shoulder, "You'll always be my *best* friend."

I shake his hand off. "Believe me, I'm *not* jealous."

"How did you end up in jail?" Evangeline interrupts, asking the question that we both want to know the answer to.

Alistair presses his lips together as if to keep the secret from spilling out, and I guarantee it's not as salacious as he thinks it is.

"I'd rather not say in front of a lady," he states in a demure tone, and looks pointedly at Evangeline.

"Don't be dramatic. It can't be any worse than this," I gesture to his outfit.

"I highly doubt that's why," Evangeline cuts in, placing her hands on her hips and looking pointedly at Alistair.

"I'll find out later and just tell her anyway," I express.

"I'll take my chances," he denotes, tight lipped. "Can we just go? People are staring."

I look around the park, but aside from the homeless man sleeping on the bench, there's only an elderly couple walking on the other side of the park feeding the geese.

"Are you afraid you're going to scare the geese?"

"Don't try to be funny, Darren," Alistair sneers.

I hold my hands up. "I wouldn't dare when clearly you do it so much better."

"Do not make me come after you." Alistair tries to sound menacing, but I just can't take him seriously while he's wearing a dress, especially since he can't seem to stay upright in his heels.

"I'd like to see you try," I laugh as Alistair glares at me.

"If I knew you were going to be such an ass, I would have called someone else."

We cross the street and reach the lot where my car is parked.

Stopping by the driver's door, I glare at him. "One of your *friends* at work?" I suggest.

"I'm worried about the two of you." Evangeline opens the back door for Alistair. When he lifts his foot to get in, she gasps and says, "Are those Louboutins?" she asks, pointing to the red bottom of Alistair's raised heel.

"What? I'm not wearing just *any* heels." Alistair shrugs as if we're both stupid. "I have standards." Then he ducks his head into the car and slams the door shut.

"*I* don't even have a pair of Louboutins."

I lean against the car admiring her. I think she's the most gorgeous creature to walk the earth. "I'll buy you a pair if you want," I offer, and she turns towards me with a surprised expression.

I would have bought her anything she wanted, but that wasn't the point. This was the decisive moment where I could try putting everything behind me, rid myself of the mental image of her with my father, block out the omission, and see only *her*, because God knows if holding onto grudges was an Olympic event, I would have a gold medal.

"Not necessary."

Instead of rounding the car, she waits… for what I don't know. I'm not good at this, apologizing *or* expressing my feelings, but I want to kiss her. To have the weight of my body press her against the car, feel her hips pushing into me, and her soft hair against my face as I bury myself in the hollow of her neck; to steady *me* instead of Alistair.

Her hand rests on the space next to the window, her fingers curl against the unyielding metal and I step forward, but the window rolls down and Alistair's head pokes out.

"Can we stop for coffee? I don't care where," he says and then pulls a face. "I retract that. Slipstream has this Ethiopian blend that's just…" he doesn't get to finish the sentence because I push his face back through the window. Evangeline laughs, lifting her hand to cover her mouth while I give her a lopsided smile. *Fucking Alistair.*

7

The Crux
Evangeline

ailey pulls the car out in front of the National Archives Museum, a large Greek-inspired building with wide stone steps that lead up to the columned entrance, making me regret wearing high-heeled boots. It's not as large as the National Portrait Museum, but it's impressive and intimidating nonetheless. Bailey senses my hesitation, his eyes meeting mine in the rearview mirror.

"The building won't bite," he teases.

"What about the people inside?" I challenge.

"That I can't guarantee," he laughs softly, "but you strike me as someone who's not afraid to bite back, so..." He trails off while unbuckling his seatbelt.

"Bailey..." I stop him before he gets out, his eyes meeting mine again in the rearview mirror.

I hesitate because I feel like I should just let it go, but the need to know is overwhelming, so I ask anyway. "Why didn't *you* say something to Darren when you recognized me?"

Bailey's shoulders sink as if he's letting out a breath. "Why didn't you tell Darren?"

"I didn't want Darren to think badly of his father. Well, any more than he already did… or me," I admit the last part quietly.

That's the crux of the situation: I *did* care what Darren thought of me and perhaps, just perhaps, that was why I was so angry at him. An anger that has faded now to almost an echo.

Bailey's quiet for a moment and I almost take it as my sign to get out, but then he speaks. "I worked for Senator Walker, not Darren."

It feels like we were both being loyal to Kerry for different reasons.

I nod, meeting his eyes in the rearview mirror one last time before he gets out to open the door for me. The wind whips my trench coat around my calves. I tighten the belt against my waist and make my way inside.

Nothing could have prepared me for the rotunda of the National Archives Museum.

When I was in elementary school, we took a field trip to the state capital in Phoenix. I remembered sitting on the bus, giddy at the fact that I didn't have to be in a classroom that day. I was going to see something important. It didn't disappoint, and maybe I was the only kid to cling to every word of our tour guide, but it was the soaring dome ceilings and the murals that gave me this feeling of being a part of something bigger.

"It's beautiful, isn't it?" Audrina Elwood catches me gaping at the murals, and I quickly close my mouth.

Her silver hair is pinned back, and she's wearing an impeccably tailored beige dress with a collar that exposes enough to see a delicate gold chain around her slender neck. She seems to blend into the room, whereas I stand out with my bold blue trench coat and black high heeled boots that are loud against the tile.

"Yes," I say, trying not to seem so… simple.

She smiles at me sweetly and takes my hand, her thumb brushing over my wedding band. "This is interesting," she says, inspecting the gold band with dice for a diamond.

I retract my hand. "Darren's an interesting man," I say.

Audrina laughs. "That is true."

We pass a large crowd of people lined up behind velvet ropes that lead to a display that I only catch a glimpse of as we pass.

"Is that the Declaration of Independence?"

"Yes, feel free to stay and look afterwards."

I crane my neck to look further, but we're too far away for me to see anything substantial.

Audrina shows the security guard her credentials, and he steps aside.

"I'm so glad you decided to be involved with the charity," she says over the noise of my loud heels hitting the tile as we make our way down the long hallway. "It was only right that a Walker be on the board, and Darren isn't cut out for charity work."

"Well, I'm not sure how much I can commit. I've never done *this* kind of charity work before," I explain.

"What *kind* have you done?" she inquires, picking up on my meaning.

"I've volunteered at a food bank for the past few Thanksgivings."

She stops in front of an office door. "That's wonderful, especially on a holiday."

She smiles and then opens the door. Behind a desk is a woman not much younger than Audrina.

"Bethany York, this is Evangeline Walker," Audrina introduces us.

She stretches out her hand. "Yes, Darren's wife, so nice to officially meet you. We didn't get a chance at the charity event."

"Very nice to meet you." As I shake her hand, I can't help

remembering the game Darren and I played at the charity event.

"Darren said you were retiring."

Bethany doesn't look old enough to retire, but I don't suppose she works here for the money. Her office is decorated with a delicate looking yellow wallpaper that brightens up the space – especially with all the dark wood furniture.

She gestures for me to take a seat on the couch adjacent to the desk.

"That's true. My tenure ends just before the holidays."

"Can I take your coat?" Audrina asks, before I take a seat.

I shrug off my coat, handing it to Audrina, and regretting my short black pleated skirt and pink cashmere sweater. I did it on purpose because I already knew what they thought of me, but so far, they've both been pleasant. At least they have Darren's best interests at heart, and I can understand the scrutiny. I'm an outsider.

"How interesting it must be to work here." I take a seat, crossing my legs and setting my purse on the floor.

"It is," she says with a melancholy tone. "And as rewarding as it has been, I'm looking forward to devoting my time to do more charity work."

Audrina takes a seat next to me on the couch.

"What do board members do?" I look between the two of them, feeling a bit foolish, but I need to know what I'm signing up for.

"We ensure the foundation is sustainable. Some of our Board members have backgrounds in ethics, finance, and law, who all help with that," Audrina explains.

"I'm afraid I don't have any of that experience. I thought it was fundraising, donations, things like that," I explain, feeling a bit dumb.

"Oh no, I didn't mean to make it sound complicated. Of course we do all of that, and Merrill was very hands on. She would personally deliver donation items to the safe houses on occasion." Audrina's expression softens at the mention of Darren's mother.

"She sounds like a wonderful woman," I say, smoothing out the creases in my skirt.

"Oh, she was," Bethany adds with a fond smile. "The Abigail Pershing Foundation was her third child."

"Kerry was considered her first child," she laughs, "and Darren of course. Merrill always put family first, but she really threw herself into making the foundation successful."

"What—" I struggle to find the words. "What happened to Abigail?"

"Darren didn't tell you anything, did he?" Audrina asks.

Bethany shakes her head. "He's like his mother in that way, the two of them were always secretive together," she declares, but with a fondness.

"Secretive?" I ask.

"Just that the two of them seemed to be in their own world when they were together, like a bubble. Merrill was always protective of him, you know, with Kerry being in the public eye," Bethany explains. "People can be cruel, especially newspapers, and they seemed to have such an interest in Darren."

"And Abigail?"

"It was in the papers, so tragic," Bethany shakes her head with a sigh.

"Abigail was working on the phones for Kerry's campaign. Merrill didn't know her husband was abusive until he came in one night looking for Abigail, making accusations." Bethany's expression is somber when she continues. "Merrill was devastated when she heard. She blamed herself."

I feel bad for asking, for bringing them back to a memory of Merrill that was unpleasant.

"She created the foundation in her name," Audrina finishes with a solemn smile, "and she didn't stop until she recruited all of us." Audrina laughs, the mood lightening. "I think she felt that was the right thing to do."

"I'm sorry, I didn't mean to bring up something painful for you."

"It's okay. I don't get to talk about Merrill much. All of the papers were interested in Kerry, which is understandable, but I wish they would have known what a magnetic person Merrill was," Bethany sighs, and I can see the regret in her eyes. That was Darren's worry as well, that all the focus was on Kerry and his mother would be forgotten. At least the foundation can be her legacy.

"Well," Bethany claps her hands together signaling the topic closed. She's thorough in her explanation of how the foundation works, and what organizations they partner with. I'm more interested in the safe houses, because that sounds like something I can really help with.

"The Board meets once a month. If you'd like to see how the operations work and where you might be able to apply your skills, we'd love to have you," Bethany offers.

"We reconvene after the holidays. I'll send you all the details," Audrina explains and then stands, signaling our meeting is over.

"Thank you. I'll be in touch," I offer, shaking Audrina's hand, but before I retrieve my coat, Bethany stops me.

"If you don't mind staying, I have something Darren said you'd be interested in," she says with a twinkle in her eyes.

8

Love Affair With Things That Could Never Be

Darren

The National Archives Museum is full of centuries worth of documents that have priceless monetary and historical value, but there is nothing in this room more valuable than Evangeline's smile. It's the kind of smile that reaches her eyes, making them an unearthly shade of blue. When they're trained on me, they make my heart stop.

"Do you like?" I gesture to the gift on the table in front of her that I enlisted Bethany's help with – priceless love letters that Emerson wrote.

The door clicks shut as I move further into the room, my attention never wavering from Evangeline's as she stands in black high heeled boots and a *very* short skirt. If she bent over, I might be able to see the crease of her heart shaped ass. I contemplate pushing the priceless Emerson letters to the ground just to watch her pick them up.

"Did you promise to let Bethany whip you if she did you this favor?" Evangeline muses.

"A gentleman never tells," I shrug.

Evangeline purses her lips. I join her at the desk where

Bethany has provided a small portion of letters that Emerson wrote to Margaret Fuller. There is a protective covering over the letters, and the room is kept dim to further aid in their preservation.

"You'd already given me a present by letting me tag along to pick up Alistair from the park police." Her voice is full of amusement.

I lift an eyebrow. "Am I not allowed to give you another?"

I study her face as she studies the letters. It's the way her hands hover over them as if she wants to gather them up and hide them under her pillow for safekeeping. It's her romanticism that I am dangerously drawn to.

"You look at those letters with a wonder that rivals history-lovers who first view the Declaration of Independence in the rotunda, and yet none of those people would travel across the country to view the conflicted love letters written by Emerson to a woman who was not his wife."

It feels as if the temperature in the room rises as she settles her gaze on me. I have to fidget with the loose change in my pocket to stop myself from grabbing her by the back of the neck and pulling her to my lips. It's been too long since I've tasted her, ran my thumb over her plump bottom lip, and I am all too eager to do just that.

"Can you really call him conflicted when he was clearly married while he wrote such beautiful letters to Margaret? I think he knew exactly what he wanted; he just couldn't have it."

"I might be coerced into thinking that you have a love affair with things that can never be."

"Aren't those the most romantic ones?" she challenges, and the tilt of her mouth has me on edge.

Everything about her has me on edge.

"What's romantic about not having what it is you crave; the very thing that keeps you up at night and invades your dreams?" I contemplate, rubbing the stubble along my jaw while struggling to keep my hands to myself.

"Spoken like a boy who was born with a silver spoon in his mouth." It's her challenging smirk that causes me to cage her against the table.

A startled breath escapes her lips. Her back arches as she looks up at me with wide blue eyes through long black lashes. She blinks against her bangs, the action so innocent but so tempting. Her perfect pink lips part as she swallows nervously, causing an ache to form in my chest.

"I take what I want," I threaten, licking my lips as I stare down at her small frame, but it's her defiant and confident attitude that makes her presence fill the room. "Is there something wrong with that?"

I will go to hell for thinking of fucking her here in this sacred place with century-old love letters, de-classified white house documents, presidential libraries, and of all things, the Declaration of Independence.

"Only if it doesn't belong to you," she challenges with that smart, kissable mouth of hers.

"Then it's a very good thing that you're mine," I rasp, my voice sounding as old and weathered as the Emerson letters. My eyes drop to her lips – full and pouty – the pink lip gloss shimmering in the dim lighting that I want to smear as I kiss her hard and deep.

The handle to the office door turns, and I take one step back from Evangeline. Her fingers grip the edge of the desk and her eyes are trained on my hand with equal amusement and heat as I discreetly try to readjust my cock so Bethany doesn't see the beginning of my hard-on.

"Darren, I see you made it. What did you think of the letters?" Bethany York asks as she enters the room, either unaware of how close I was to fucking Evangeline on those letters – or pretending not to notice.

She collects her white gloves from the desk and slides them on to handle the documents.

"Inspiring," I confirm, cocking my head to the side while still staring at Evangeline, who stares back with amusement.

Her cheeks flush as she turns towards Bethany.

"Your wife is very charming," Bethany declares as she gathers the letters.

I clear my throat and finish adjusting myself while Bethany's back is to me.

"When Darren told me it would please you greatly to see the Emerson letters, well," she pauses and turns to me, "I couldn't say no."

Evangeline hesitates, and I sense the conflict in her eyes, the way she fights to keep little pieces of herself hidden. "I was a literature major in college."

"The pursuit of the arts is always a noble one," Bethany declares, giving me a wink. "Emerson obviously thought so."

Evangeline laughs. "Not everyone sees it that way."

"It's no more noble than graduating Georgetown Law top of their class," Bethany directs her accusatory eyes towards me.

"Thank you, but we don't want to keep you any longer." Evangeline grabs her jacket from the rack by the door. "I'm sure you have better things to do than indulge my fascination with Emerson."

"It's my pleasure. Anything for Darren." She gives me a knowing smile and then turns to Evangeline. "We'll be in touch about the foundation."

"Thank you, Bethany." I give her a chaste kiss on the cheek and then take Evangeline's hand, leading her from the room and back down the long hallway towards the rotunda.

"You were charming?" I tease.

"I can behave, Darren. Your lack of confidence is disappointing."

"This outfit says otherwise." My eyes drop to her short skirt.

"You don't like?" She flicks the hem.

"I like it very much."

When we reach the door at the end of the long hallway, I clear my throat and turn towards her.

"Thank you." I don't say it often enough, and aim to rectify that.

Evangeline tilts her head. "I should be thanking *you*. You didn't have to do that."

"I know how much it means to you, and it would be selfish of me to deny you when it's within my power."

Her eyes turn a deeper shade of blue, and her lips part.

"You seem to have a lot of influence, Darren Walker."

"When you have enough money…"

"No," she interrupts, "it's not because of your money."

I'd say she's looking at me with admiration, but I know better. No, it's more like understanding, the kind of understanding when someone sees deep down inside of you, and it's unnerving.

"Why were you thanking me earlier?" she asks.

"For running interference with Bethany," I explain.

"For someone so narcissistic, you don't take compliments well," she teases.

It's that smart mouth that brings back the ache deep in my belly.

"It's clear Bethany adores you," she adds.

"People would always say I had my father's charm and wit. It felt more like a burden than a compliment."

"And now?"

I drag in a deep breath. "It reminds me of what I didn't finish," I admit.

"Why didn't you take the Bar exam?"

If I could give her the answer I've given countless people – the polite answer, the bullshit answer – I would.

"Hope should be something that fills you up and carries you forward, but for me, it felt like an anchor. I was on this path that had been mapped out for me since I was born, and that's a heavy burden to live up to."

I don't know if I'm explaining myself correctly.

"I know how pretentious that sounds, but…" I pause, "there are so many what if's – what if I don't pass? Worse yet, what if I do?"

"What if you do pass?" she prompts. "Would that be so bad?"

"The attention I got when my father ran for office was alarming, and they'd just dug up a bad report card. Can you imagine what it would be like for me if I actually tried and failed?" I admit.

"Failure isn't a crime, Darren," she shakes her head, "but aiming low is."

I tilt my head down towards hers. "If that's true, then I am the worst kind of criminal."

She stops me by placing a finger against my lips, and it feels like an electric shock running through my body. I want to open my mouth to take a bite.

Every instinct in me screams to press her against the wall so she can feel what she does to me, to grip her hip, and lift her leg to curl around me, reminding her of the way we fit together so easily.

She removes her finger and takes a step back and it leaves me restless.

"What are you thinking?" I'm desperate to know.

"You're a very complex person, Darren, and I wonder how many people have actually been able to figure you out?"

"Have you?" I ask.

Her eyes search mine. "Why did you have Bethany show me the Emerson letters?"

"It would seem masochistic, wouldn't it?"

"Under the circumstances, yes." She tilts her head, and I track the strands of hair that fall over her shoulder.

"I want to believe that when you look at me, you don't see my father," I explain, "because that is the common thread that binds us, isn't it?" I ask, but I'm not looking for an answer. "And what a precarious thread it is." I tug on the end of her sweater, pulling her an inch closer to me. "One pull, and everything unravels." My eyes meet hers.

Her lips part, the gloss shining in the dim lighting of the hallway.

"I have the means to fly you to Paris, buy you a closet full of designer gowns, jewels, whatever the hell you want, but this…" I point down the hall and sigh, "do you know how much I want to hate Emerson? And yet I can't." I run a hand through my hair in frustration.

"Why?" she asks, touching my arm, and I can feel the heat from it pierce right through my jacket.

"Because of you," I admit. "I asked for the truth, and you gave it to me. Do you want me to punish you for it?"

"No, but Darren, you don't have to do those things for me," she pleads.

How do I explain something I can't even understand myself?

"But I do." I let out a frustrated breath. "Because one day you will look at me, and you won't see him."

The door opens and Bernie, the security guard, peers in. "You have fifteen minutes," he says.

9

Declaration of Independence

Darren

We step inside and as spectacular as it is, there's something about her in this room that rivals the Faulkner murals that grace the rounded walls of the rotunda.

"Fifteen minutes for what?" she inquires.

"The museum is closed for a private event," I explain, and looks around as if she's just now noticing how empty the rotunda is. "We have fifteen minutes before Bernie has to kick us out." I hook my thumb in the direction of the security guard who stands in front of the private entrance we just came from. His back is turned, giving us privacy.

"Bernie, huh?" Her voice is laced with amusement.

"Yes." I walk tentatively beside her with my hands clasped behind my back as she makes her way to the display.

It is the magnitude, and the notoriety of the document that draws out this trepidation inside of me, and I feel it in Evangeline too as we slowly walk across the room, stopping just short of being able to peer in.

She looks around the room and I can see how this could be

67

intimidating, but even more so are Bethany and Audrina in the same room together.

"You don't have to be part of the foundation."

"I want to," she says quickly.

"I know Audrina especially can be a bit much."

"They both care about you a lot." We stand face to face. Her expression holds a secret I wish I was privy to.

"They were my mother's oldest friends," I explain. "Hopefully they were nice to you."

"That's why you didn't give Audrina my number, isn't it? You were afraid they'd call me a gold digger and chase me off?"

"Please tell me they did not do that," I plead, embarrassed.

She shakes her head. "I've been called worse," she says too easily. I have been guilty of doing just that.

She turns away from me and peers into the display case while I dutifully hold her jacket.

Her fingers skim over the glass as if applying any more pressure would break it. "Is this real?" she questions nervously.

"Do you think they would put out a fake?" I ask with amusement.

"It wouldn't be the first time our government lied to us," she says cheekily. "But aren't they worried about something happening to it? Wouldn't they want to store it away to keep it safe?"

I step forward to meet her, but instead of looking at the document, my eyes stay trained on her. "It belongs to the people, not the National Archives Museum or the government for that matter. Besides, it's well protected." I tilt my head toward Bernie who still has his back to us, but no doubt an ear tuned in our direction.

"The day after the attack on Pearl Harbor, it was packed

up and sent to Fort Knox, along with the Constitution and the Magna Carta."

"My own personal tour guide?" She peers back down into the glass case.

"If you're interested…"

"I am," she says eagerly, cutting me off.

"This isn't the only copy," I point out, and that piques her interest. "There were approximately two hundred of them printed, but only twenty-six are still in existence today, three of which are privately owned." I scratch the back of my head and she looks at me with interest.

"I can't imagine having something like that in my home, no matter how much money I had."

"They're called Dunlap Broadsides. Back then they were hand printed, meaning every single letter was a wooden piece that had to be handset. So, on some of the prints, there were punctuation marks missing, and even whole words. Each one is different." I realize that I'm talking way too much because she's staring at me, so I stop.

"What?" I prod nervously.

"This is your Emerson, isn't it?" she contemplates.

I peer into the case, noticing how the original ink is so faded you can barely make out the words, but I don't need to see them on a piece of paper because they are ingrained in my mind. "We hold these truths to be self-evident, that all men are created equal, that they are endowed by their creator certain unalienable Rights, that among these are Life, Liberty, and the Pursuit of Happiness," I recite with my eyes trained on her the whole time. "If *that* is not poetry, then I don't know what is."

"You make it sound so beautiful."

"Each man that signed this document did so with a fear for his life, so yes, there is beauty and courage in one's conviction for doing something difficult, and at the time, very unpopular."

"You really love history," she observes.

"Not just history, but specifically this because it is the cata-lyst for the U.S. Constitution which is the very basis for law, and by extension, the protection of," I explain hastily. "I've seen it many times, from childhood field trips to a curious adult, and the emotions it evokes never lessens." I dare to look at her for fear that I've rambled too much and possibly bored her.

"And yet, you're not a lawyer," she counters. "I would think that if you're so moved by it, you would be able to set aside your pride to protect it."

"My pride?"

"Isn't that what you said earlier?" she reminds me. "You *take* what you want."

"Pride can either make you soar or ground you." I have been grounded so long that I don't remember what it feels like to fly. "If I tried and failed, then what?"

She shrugs which isn't an agreement, nor is it a contradic-tion, and I think it's her indifference that makes me pull at the collar of my shirt.

"If you don't try, then you'll never know."

When she bends over to look inside the case, I swear she does it on purpose because she knows that her skirt lifts enough to reveal the crease of her ass that I was so fixated on earlier in the reading room. It's not just the soft roundness of exposed flesh that I see, it's the hint of a G-string underneath that sets my pulse racing, the tiny strand of black cotton threaded through her ass cheeks.

I know it's deliberate when she looks back at me, strands of her long blonde hair caressing the glass that holds the most important piece of our nation's history, and I don't care that she's taunting me.

"Evangeline," I grit out a warning and that defiant, taunting smile of hers will be the death of me. "Do you want me to go to jail for public indecency?" I warn through gritted teeth.

She straightens, looking at me with those not so innocent eyes and says, "I doubt it would be the first time."

I stand next to her, my fingers discretely inching their way up the back of her thigh and under her skirt to feel the warm, soft roundness of her ass, and she invites me in by parting her legs further. I run my finger along the slit of her cunt, feeling the wetness that is already starting to pool against the thin fabric of her panties. I groan in response.

"You're right, but the first time wouldn't be as worth it as this."

"You'll have to tell me the story," she whispers, and then rewards me with a small moan as I cup her pussy, one finger pressing firmly on the bud of her clit.

I lean in close, looking down at her, my eyes traveling over her parted lips. "Perhaps if you're a good girl, I will."

"Darren Walker," she slides her hand over my growing cock, and even through the fabric of my jeans it is tantalizing enough to cause my balls to draw tight and my stomach to quiver. "We only have fifteen minutes, and I think we've taken up about ten of those."

"That sounds like a challenge," I rasp. "Do you doubt that I could make you come in under five?" I challenge, draping the trench coat around her shoulders. The feel of her trembling thigh against the back of my hand makes me want to bend her over right here.

"Perhaps if we're quiet, I'd let you fuck me right here," she taunts, her fingers skimming over glass that holds the Declaration of Independence. "Bernie looks to be hard of hearing," she teases.

"Silent is not how I fuck," I whisper in her ear as I slip my fingers under her skirt again.

The sound of her broken breath is enough to make me come in my pants, especially feeling the flimsy, soaked fabric of her panties, and every wet fold of her layers underneath.

She leans into me, resting her forehead to my chest, short breaths escaping her lips and her fingers curling around the hem of my shirt. I wish I could set her down on the display, part her thighs, and kneel before her so I could sink my tongue into her bare, wet cunt.

The indecent thoughts fuel my need to make her come, to hear her whimper and beg against my chest. I increase the pressure of my thumb on her clit, and I know I've hit the right spot when the trembling of her thighs intensifies.

"Darren," she whispers in a panic, her earlier bravado fading. Her voice is broken and faded, much like the document that sits underneath the glass mere inches from where we stand. "I can't..." she begs breathlessly, peering over my shoulder.

"This is what you wanted," I whisper in her ear while she begins to fall apart. "This is why you wore this skirt and those panties, to tempt me," I remind her gruffly.

It's not just her short skirt or her cunt gripping my fingers, it's her pouty lips, and her moans that sound like church bells that make me a deviant; the kind of man who prays at the altar of the Constitution, and yet, here I am, defiling one of America's greatest documents because of her.

I grip the back of her neck, pulling her closer, letting her lean against me as her body wilts heavily with desire. "So, you can, and you will, Queenie," I rasp just before I pull her mouth to mine, capturing her cries as her orgasm crests, right before the iron gates are unlocked and a group of patrons are let into the rotunda.

To them, we might look like a pair of lovers overcome with emotion, slouched together and murmuring whispered sentiments about viewing the document instead of a desperate man who just gave his wife an orgasm in under five minutes.

Evangeline's eyes flutter open a fraction as the group nears us. She watches as I inhale her scent on my finger, wishing I could taste her. She presses her skirt back down and I close the gap of her trench coat, securing the belt like a doting husband. I smile at the unsuspecting group as I take Evangeline's hand and lead her outside to the steps where Bailey is waiting at the curb with the car. I haven't gone down a flight of stairs this fast since I was a child, and the minute we're safely tucked into the back of the sedan with the privacy window up, I turn to Evangeline and say, "Now, be a good wife and sit on my face."

10

Confession
Evangeline

*I*t's still dark out, and when I look at the alarm clock on the bedside table, morning is still a long way off. I turn slowly so as not to wake Darren and burrow myself against his warm chest.

The cold, antique couch in the front room must be lonely tonight without him draped across its uncomfortable cushions.

He moans deeply, and I feel the vibration against my cheek. His arms tighten around me, but he doesn't say anything. Only the slow, lazy circles he draws on my back let me know he's awake. We're a tangle of arms and legs under the blankets. Even with the heater on, the house is still drafty and cold.

His fingers dance up my back and push the hair off my shoulder so he can lean down to press a kiss on the top of my shoulder, and his lips linger as if he's fallen back asleep.

We came home from the museum, went to bed, and never came out.

He may pretend not to care about anything, but deep

below the murky golds and greens of his eyes lies a man with a deep passion for history with a poet's heart, even if he doesn't think so himself.

Perhaps I find it hard to sleep because my conscience is weighing heavily upon me. I don't want there to be anymore secrets between us, and Darren deserves to know the truth.

I dig my fingers into his chest and feel his body wake up in response. The admission is on my tongue like sour candy, and if I don't say it now, I don't think I'll have the courage later.

"My mother's alive," I whisper, and feel the playful circles falter against my back like the skipping of a record.

All I hear is his breathing and the soft patter of rain against the windowpane. I'd give anything to know what he's thinking, and every second of silence is killing me because Darren isn't one to usually hold his tongue.

"I know."

I push away from him enough so that I can see his face. He stares at me, but there's no anger in his eyes.

Of course he knew. A man with resources such as Darren's would definitely have looked into my past, especially before he married me. I can hardly be mad about it. "You let me lie."

He sighs, his voice still heavy with sleep. "I figured you had a good reason."

I stare at the fine hairs that dust his chest and count the freckles caused by too many lazy days spent in the sun.

When I venture to look at his face again. His eyes are closed, but I know he hasn't fallen back asleep. He cups the back of my head and pulls me closer to him, his body curling around mine.

"You're not upset with me?" I ask into his chest.

"Aren't we done being angry with each other?" His voice is quiet and hoarse like the sound of kindling firewood.

"That's not good enough, Darren."

"Lies aren't equal, Evan. There's no one keeping score.

And when it comes to parents, I have enough understanding – especially when it's about *your* parents – not mine."

The heaviness in my chest only expands, and his words threaten to unravel me. "I said she was dead because it was easier than admitting she knew what I did for a living."

"I don't want you to feel like you have to hide from me anymore."

I take a deep breath, inhaling the familiar scent of his cologne.

"I don't remember my father," I admit. "I was really young when he died."

Darren tucks my head further into the crook of his neck, resting his chin against me.

"His death changed my mother, but I didn't notice until there was no going back and I didn't recognize her anymore."

Darren remains quiet. The pattern he draws along my shoulder blade is the only thing grounding me.

"We lived with my grandparents, and after my grandpa died, my mother remarried." I can feel my voice start to waver, but I press on. "I was a teenager by then." I have to take a deep breath.

"My grandmother had already been diagnosed with MS and she was deteriorating swiftly," I explain.

What I have to say next… I'm glad that I don't have to look at him because I'm already on the verge of letting my emotions get the better of me. I've been so good at hiding things that I didn't know if I could find them again.

"I didn't like the way he looked at me, and my grandmother must have sensed it too, because I would sometimes find her in the morning still asleep in her recliner just off the hallway to my bedroom."

Darren's body stiffens, his fingers pausing the lazy circles on my back.

"Hmm," his chest rumbles against my ear. "You shouldn't tell me things like that," he rasps.

I tilt my head to finally look at him. His lips part, but his eyes remain closed.

"Why?"

His hand moves from my back to run the pad of his thumb over my cheek without even looking at me.

"I am not a violent man," he says with a voice that is rough and deep. Then he opens his eyes and tips his chin down to level his gaze upon me. "But I would do unspeakable things for you."

I pull the refrigerator door open and peer inside, trying to decide if I'm hungry or not. I grab a yogurt when I hear the doorbell ring.

When I open the door, Rausch is standing on the front porch. The look on his face tells me he was expecting Darren, not me. This time I'm wearing Darren's Georgetown t-shirt and a pair of sweatpants. Maybe he thought Darren sent me packing, accomplished what he set out to do with those photos — get rid of me.

My emotions are still raw, and seeing him is like scratching at an exposed nerve. Everything I thought I had made peace with seems to come back to the surface. Without saying a word, I step onto the porch and slap him.

The sound cuts through the silence of the early morning sleepy neighborhood like a whip. The indignant look on Rausch's face should cause me to take a step back, but I don't. Whatever he has to give, I can take it.

"What did you think you would accomplish by giving Darren those photos?" I raise my voice.

Rausch's gaze settles back on me, his steely blue eyes narrowed.

"I gather Darren didn't take it well?" he asks with an expectant expression.

"You humiliated me."

"I don't know you," he states bluntly, "and I don't owe you anything, so your feelings are not my concern."

He's right, he doesn't owe me anything. We only know each other because of circumstance. I study his large form that takes up the bulk of the doorway, impeccably dressed even in this early hour of the day.

I'm good at judging character – a skill acquired because of my profession – but Rausch has always been a difficult read. "You knew nothing happened between us." I narrow my eyes and search his face for any indication that I'm right, and the tick in his jaw confirms it. "You just wanted him to think it did."

"I have known this family for longer than you have been alive, and you've been here, what," he looks at his gold watch to make his point, "five minutes?"

"You didn't have to go about it the way you did." I allow my outrage to seep into my tone.

"Young lady," Rausch responds condescendingly, "there is no room for consideration of feelings in politics. You're lucky *I* was the one to give the photos to Darren, because if I hadn't, they would have ended up in the paper under *much* different circumstances," he admits.

He acts like I should be grateful for his intervention.

"You got them from Langley. Kerry died, and the pictures became irrelevant, until Darren punched Langley at the charity event." Which I'm sure wasn't good for his ego.

Rausch doesn't confirm my suspicion, and his face remains as stoic as ever. Regardless, I'm sure he knows what kind of man Langley is without me having to tell him. The fact that Langley had those photos all this time makes my skin crawl, even more than when his hands were on me.

"You have no idea how many fires I've had to put out

because of her," Rausch states, looking next to me as I feel Darren's arm wrap around my waist.

"I didn't ask you to protect me," Darren expresses.

Rausch laughs. "It's not *you* I'm protecting."

I can feel Darren's fingers dig into my side as if he's trying to stop himself from lunging at Rausch. I could tell him it's not worth it, but slapping him felt better than I expected.

His expression softens infinitesimally. "I would never let Kerry's reputation be tarnished," he admits.

"While I don't doubt that, I think you also didn't want to miss the opportunity to prove me wrong and try to put a wedge between me and Evangeline."

Rausch's eyes travel down to where Darren's hand rests at my waist.

I can tell it bothers him, and I delight in the fact that it does.

"I'm good at my job, Darren, especially the ugly parts," he explains. "Politics is a dirty game, and anyone who says otherwise is a fool. Your father knew that best."

"I know you didn't come for a social call, so tell me, to what do we owe this pleasure?" Darren inquires through pressed lips.

"Well, Darren, there was never a question about your intelligence." Rausch reaches into his jacket and pulls out an envelope.

"Last time you gave me an envelope, it wasn't so pleasant."

"And what did you do with the other information I gave you?" he asks rather sheepishly, which is uncommon for Rausch.

"I think you like riddles, but I have better things to do than play games."

I can see the amusement in Rausch's eyes, but whatever he's thinking, he doesn't give it away. Instead, he hands Darren the envelope.

"This is the report for the investigation into your parents helicopter crash," Rausch announces solemnly. "I wanted you to be the first to know because *The Post* will be printing an article tomorrow."

He takes it with trepidation.

"I also wanted to let you know that Georgetown would like to name their new non-profit law clinic after your parents," he declares. "They would like you to attend."

Darren looks uncomfortable, and I know speaking in public is not his favorite thing.

"You mean Walker," he confirms with disdain.

"When the University President first approached me, I made it clear that it should be both your parents."

Darren's eyes widen, and he nods before closing the door.

11

Envelopes Are Not My Friend

Darren

cup of coffee and a plate of food is left discarded on the counter while I bury my head in Evangeline's lap as she threads her fingers through my hair.

"What was Rausch talking about, when he asked about the other information he'd given you?"

I sigh but understand her trepidation given Rausch's reputation.

I lift my head and stand up straight, but I don't let go of her. Instead, I settle my body between her legs as her feet dangle off the counter.

"I asked Rausch about my grandfather."

She gives me an inquisitive look while her hands rest on my shoulders and her thighs squeeze against my hips.

"After the funeral when he had my grandfather escorted away," I refresh her memory.

"Escorted is too nice a description." She quirks one side of her mouth.

"When I asked him about it, I believe he gave some

cryptic answer like *even your father didn't tell me everything,*" I explain in a mocking tone, trying to sound like him.

"That is the worst impression of Rausch," she teases.

I shrug, happy that I *don't* sound like him. "I guess my career as a comedian is over."

She smiles, and it's impossible not to smile right along with her, though this doesn't feel like a particularly happy moment.

"All he gave me was a police report from thirty years ago, and who the fuck knows if my grandfather still lives there," I say frustrated, and realizing how awkward the word 'grandfather' feels rolling off my tongue.

"You didn't want to look into it?" she asks curiously, while she traces a pattern on my chest.

My eyes meet hers. "I was preoccupied with other things," I remind her.

"So, you can see why envelopes are not my friend these days." I plant a kiss on her exposed shoulder.

Her skin smells clean and floral, with the hint of cherry blossoms that makes this house more like a home than I have ever known. It's almost enough to make me forget, but the thick brown envelope is staring at me and so I move away reluctantly to gather it up.

Ripping it open, I pull out the report and begin skimming through it.

"They're prosecuting the pilot," I say almost to myself. "There's a lot of technical stuff in here that I don't understand, but they believe the pilot to be negligent."

I throw the envelope down on the counter. "The flight from Virginia isn't even that long, and…" I press my lips together thinking of how many times I'd taken that ride with them.

"They were coming back from their home in Virginia?" Evangeline inquires, sliding off the counter and grabbing my discarded plate of breakfast that she'd been so kind to make after Rausch left, but then I quickly lost my appetite thinking about what was in the report. It's not like knowing the cause makes this any better, but anger licks at the edges of my mind, thinking that technical skill could have avoided the crash.

"They have a place in the country," I explain, right before she stabs a piece of egg and holds it to my lips.

"I'm not a child, you know?" I complain absently.

"I know," she soothes, still holding the fork in front of me until I pull the piece of egg off and eat it.

"Did you go there a lot?" she questions.

"When I was a kid, we went all the time," I affirm. "We drove back then. I hated being in the car that long with nothing to do."

"No games of *I Spy?*" she giggles.

I look up at her and give a small chuckle, placing my hands on her hips. "We did." I had forgotten about that.

"When my father started his campaign our life became chaotic, and then I went to boarding school so we only made it for the occasional holiday," I sigh as she holds another forkful of egg out to me, but instead of complaining I just eat it like a good boy.

"That must have been nice to have a place like that," Evangeline muses, while I hook my thumbs under the waistband of her sweatpants and drag her closer. She makes a startled squeal.

"I don't like these." I tug on her pants, making a face.

She smiles, playfully pulling away. "Too bad, it's cold. Did you like going there?" she prods me further.

I furrow my brows, and it's not an unpleasant thought that crosses my mind; quite on the contrary. "He wasn't Senator Kerry Walker there," I admit. "He was just my dad. He took me hunting," I chuckle at the thought. "I remember he told me that he used to go turkey hunting in the spring with his brothers when he was younger." That was probably the only thing he said to me about growing up.

"I didn't want him to be disappointed in me, so I went, but he could tell I didn't like it," I admit. "I think the Republican in him died a little bit when he found out his son didn't like guns," I chuckle at the memory.

She grabs a piece of bacon and holds it out to me. "Did he hold it against you?"

"No," I reply, shaking my head. "He never said anything, but instead of hunting, we would go for walks in the woods and he'd make a game of trying to figure out what kind of animal prints were in the dirt." I smile at the memory.

I lean forward and take a bite of the bacon from her hand as if I'm a dog getting a treat, my teeth gently grazing her fingers. "We should go," I exclaim while chewing.

"Where?" she asks, while brushing the remnants of bacon off her hands and cleaning up the rest of our plates, apparently satisfied with what I've eaten.

"To Virginia, the lake house. We can have Thanksgiving there." I never thought I'd be excited at the thought of going to my parent's lake house, but the timing is right. "I think it'll be good to get out of the city," I beam, looking at her expectantly. "And I need to check on it before winter." I scratch the back of my head.

Evangeline starts loading the dishwasher. "You know you don't have to do that." I gesture to the dirty dishes in the sink.

"I'm not leaving this for Lottie." She bumps the door closed with her hip and stares at me.

"So, what's your parents lake house like?" She leans against the counter, wiping her hands on a towel.

"It's a log cabin in the woods near the lake. You'll like it. Lots of open space. There's a trail along the lake where you can run if the weather holds out long enough," I explain.

"Sounds quaint," she smiles, tossing the towel on the counter.

12

Everything In Due Time

Darren

"You didn't tell me that Langley was presenting the plaque!" We pass the Quad into the heart of Georgetown University.

"I didn't tell you because I knew you wouldn't come," Rausch grits his teeth.

"You're fucking right I wouldn't."

"Keep your voice down, Darren," he scolds me. "Sometimes you have to put your personal feelings aside for such an occasion."

"My personal feelings? This isn't a schoolyard tiff, Rausch."

"He was your father's friend, and a colleague in the Senate. The University asked him, and it would have raised questions if you refused," Rausch explains.

"You know I don't care about perception."

"You don't need to remind me of that," Rausch groans behind a fake smile as the university president approaches us.

"Everything in due time, Darren," Rausch laments in a

low voice while plastering a smile on his face, and I do the same.

"We're honored to have you here today." The university president extends his hand for me to shake.

I never met him before. Georgetown wasn't like boarding school where indiscretions warranted a trip to the Dean's office.

"I was very sorry to hear about your parents passing." He lets go of my hand while the courtyard begins to fill, and chatter echoes off the stone walkways.

"Thank you," I say politely.

"The university thought this was the best way to honor *both* your father and mother, who were distinguished alumnus." He gestures to the Law Alumni Lounge, which has been transformed into a non-profit law clinic bearing my last name: Walker Memorial Law Clinic. "Especially with such a large donation to the University," he explains.

There is one thing my father was proud of, and that was his legacy – the work he did as a lawyer to help people. When I look at the clinic, I feel a lump in my throat, a feeling of immense pride that takes me by surprise.

I try to ignore the shame that blooms inside me as I look around at this University that I had taken advantage of, and dare I say… squandered.

I clear my throat. "I can speak for both of them when I say they would have been honored."

When he starts to explain the sequence of events, the ceremony of cutting the ribbon, a commemorative plaque presentation – the mention of Jonathan Langley curdling my stomach – I tune him out, especially when I know Rausch is taking notes like a teacher's pet.

In the distance I catch a glimpse of Evangeline, her attention focused on the expansive courtyard boxed in by buildings with stone paths weaving their way around campus.

"Will you excuse me?" I interrupt him.

"Darren!" I hear Rausch calling after me, but I pay him no mind as I take my place next to her.

"It's much more beautiful in spring when the tulips bloom," I entreat.

"It looks like it belongs in a Jane Austen novel," she laughs, gesturing to the gothic style building, a spire peeking out and lifting to the clear blue sky.

I look around the courtyard and remember the first time I set foot on the campus.

"And to think it was nearly extinguished by the Civil War." I tuck my hands inside the pockets of my jacket, the chilly fall air carried in from the Potomac whips between the buildings. "Most of the students enlisted," I raise my eyebrows, "both Union and Confederate forces."

"Is that something they teach you during orientation?" she teases.

"Along with the Hoyas fight song," I tease back.

"What *is* a Hoya? Some kind of mystical animal?" she jests.

"I assure you it's nothing as exciting as that. It's derived from Hoya Saxa," I explain.

"What does it mean?"

"The literal translation is 'what rocks'."

She adjusts the lapels of my wool jacket, pulling them tighter around my chest. "You look very handsome." She smooths down an errant piece of hair from my forehead. "You wouldn't want anything to mar that."

"Is this your way of asking me to behave?" I ponder, noticing her gaze over my shoulder towards the podium.

"It looks like you're being summoned."

"Rausch is probably having heart palpitations right now," I laugh.

"You better go then."

"If I didn't know any better, I'd think you're taking enjoyment at my discomfort at having to make a public appearance."

She loops her arm through mine and we walk towards the chairs that have been set up.

"Perhaps you're very good at pretending to hate these things."

She stops at the row where a place card rests on the seat with her name on it.

"I would enjoy it better if Langley weren't giving the plaque," I grouse through gritted teeth. "If I had known ahead of time, I wouldn't have accepted." Anger slicks over my skin at just the thought of his hands on her.

"Don't let him taint something that will help a lot of people."

"I think your charitable nature is rubbing off on me. Alistair would be appalled," I joke, and that garners me a laugh.

I place a kiss on the top her head before I make my way to the front where Rausch's furrowed brow threatens to make me turn back around.

While Dr. Baines stands at the podium and makes introductions, Rausch leans closer to me and whispers in my ear, "Don't do anything stupid."

"You're lack of faith in me is disappointing. I'm a grown up, Rausch." I smooth out the lapels of my coat while staring towards the other side of the courtyard where Jonathan Langley stands.

"That's debatable, Darren. Just remember why you're here – for your parents."

"Help me in welcoming a distinguished member of Congress, Senator Jonathan Langley." Dr. Baines steps aside and I watch as Langley walks toward the podium, waving to the small camera crew that's covering the dedication.

No doubt Rausch can feel me stiffen beside him, anger wafting off me like the earthy algae smell of the nearby

Potomac, and he clears his throat as if to provide a reminder to behave.

I was never good at behaving though, so when Langley finishes his speech about working alongside my father, and how much my mother gave back to the community, I stride across the stone pathway towards him with a determined look.

He holds the plaque out to me with one hand and the other outstretched to shake mine. I stare at it, and knowing what I know about him, I think about spitting on it, but instead take it firmly – maybe a little too firmly. Perhaps it's funny since Langley has a few good inches on me. Granted, I might be a little bit bigger than I was in college, but youth is on my side.

I shake his hand rather vigorously, while I lean and say, "Looks like your nose healed nicely."

He looks towards the flashing cameras, a politician's smile plastered on his face, and I wonder how in the world anyone couldn't see past it. "You certainly made your parents proud marrying a prostitute." He grabs hold of my forearm and pulls me in further as if to give me a hug.

I can feel the anger burn through me as I grip his hand even tighter, fighting to hold on even though my palms are sweating.

"What did you think you would accomplish by releasing those photos, ruining my father's reputation by making the public think he cheated on my mother with Evangeline?" I accuse nastily, trying my best to keep a smile. "Were you just jealous that you had to hire her so she'd be in the same room with you?"

"Did she tell you my fingers were in her cunt? She was practically begging for it." So help me God, it takes everything inside of me not to punch him right here in front of everyone.

He pulls me in closer, whispering in my ear. "I was never

in competition with your father, especially when it came to that. Rausch knows that better than anyone. He and your father were very close, weren't they?" He looks over my shoulder.

"He was a better friend than you," I retort through gritted teeth even though I'm a bit confused by his accusations.

Langley rips his hand from mine. "Sure, if you want to call it that."

I take the plaque as Langley stalks off, but not without taking the opportunity to give a wave and a smile to the cameras. I'm left in front of the podium bewildered and sweaty. I can feel everyone's eyes on me, but I manage to focus on the plaque.

This honor is bestowed upon Kerry Walker and Merrill Compton-Walker for their distinguished service in law and community.

Remembering why I'm here, I turn to look at the clinic, a red ribbon stretched across its door just waiting to be ceremoniously cut.

Clearing my throat, I manage to say, "My mother would politely accept this honor with grace and remind you that our lives are not measured by what we have, but by what we give."

I look to my left where Rausch stands at the side of the makeshift stage. His proudful eyes bore into me.

"I was trying to think of what my father would say if he were here to accept this honor, but he would probably bore you with one of his speeches about Emerson and politics. He was always good at veering off topic, which I suppose I inherited from him – probably one of the only things I inherited." The crowd laughs.

In order to ground myself, I look out at the crowd and lock eyes with Evangeline.

"You might ask what Emerson has to do with politics or

even law for that matter, and my father would simply say – everything – leaving you to ponder and wanting more. He was always good about making you want more."

I take a deep breath.

"I think I know what he meant." I hear people shifting in their seats. "And perhaps I am more like my father than I thought, because I will leave you with this – *It is not the length of life, but the depth,*" I grip the podium tightly, "and both my parents lived deeply."

13

I'm No Lady
Evangeline

"I spy something blue."

"I don't want to play anymore," Darren grumbles with a petulant tone.

"That's because you've lost the last three rounds," I tease, watching as he grips the steering wheel with obvious annoyance, which is actually quite cute.

"I think you're cheating," he accuses. "And you're trying to distract me."

I sit up and drop my feet from the dash. "I do not cheat!"

"There's no other explanation," Darren declares, shaking his head and taking a brief moment to peer over at me.

I press a palm to my chest. "I am deeply offended." I flop back into my seat while Darren chuckles. "And is it working?" I lift an eyebrow.

"I won't dignify you with what Langley said to me at the dedication," Darren laments.

"Then don't, and stop thinking about it."

"He said he was never in competition with my father," he scoffs. "What a lie."

"Darren," I warn.

"Yes, dear." He bats his eyelashes at me, and I turn his face back to the road.

"Just concentrate on driving. By the way, are we almost there?" I ask.

"It's the same answer I gave you five minutes ago," he says with an annoyed tone.

"Yeah, yeah." I wave him off.

We've been in the car for nearly four hours, and the countless games of *I Spy*, and *guess what the vanity plate says*, have run their course, especially since traffic has thinned, leaving behind big cities the further south we go. I've never been in this part of the country, and I watch as the scenery passes, with its rolling green hills and deep green forests.

I can see the tilt of his lip while he concentrates on driving and place my socked feet back on the dash, daring him to protest or push them off.

The sign up ahead points towards Clarksville as Darren exits the highway, turning onto a two-lane road that passes an old gas station and a few scattered houses before driving over a long bridge to get into downtown. The street is lined with stores on both sides. It looks like one of those quaint towns that you only see in movies, with brick buildings and green awnings with names like *Sara's Stationary*, and *Bella's Bloom's*, written on them.

Even though Darren slows to a near crawl, it only takes what feels like a minute to reach the end of the block, and I crane my neck to read the sign on one of the stores, *The Sweetest Secret*.

"My mom used to take me there for ice cream in the summers," Darren sighs, the store winking out of view as he turns the corner.

"It looks cute." I turn back to Darren.

"I'll take you there once we get settled," Darren promises with a wan smile, and I'm eager to explore, but more eager to get out of the car because I'm tired of sitting for so long.

"Just like you promised to stop in Richmond so I could see the Edger Allen Poe Museum?"

"I missed the turn!"

"Liar."

"Okay, you got me. I have no desire to see a museum dedicated to a man with terminal paranoia," he spouts.

"But it's *Edgar Allen Frickin' Poe*!" I state, waving my hands in the air in frustration.

"Has anyone told you that you talk with your hands too much? I thought that was a Jersey thing."

"How's this for a hand gesture?" I give him the middle finger.

He laughs and shakes his head. "That's not very ladylike."

"I think you know by now, Darren, that I'm no lady." I smile wickedly, and Darren licks his lips while gripping the steering wheel tighter.

We turn down a back road into a heavily wooded area full of tall pines, and glimpses of water glittering like diamonds between the tree trunks. It's only a short drive before I can see a house up ahead. When the road curves and the trees open to give me a full view of the house, I realize it doesn't live up to Darren's description.

"That's not a log cabin." I point at the house with my mouth shamelessly gaping open.

"There're logs," Darren comments flippantly, as he pulls into the drive.

"Yeah, there're logs, but that's far from a cabin. I pictured something that looked like an outhouse," I tease.

Darren laughs. "Kerry and Merrill Walker staying in an outhouse?" He makes a face. "Now that would be something," he muses.

As soon as Darren stops the car, I open the door and step out. The house is made of wood logs, but there's also a portico with large wood beams and stone walls that are offset by an interesting green metal roof. I thought the Georgetown house was beautiful, but this property is... magical.

"It's amazing." I grab my bag from Darren, following him to the front door.

He stops at the threshold, as if there's an invisible barrier preventing him from stepping inside. I peer past him and spot an open book and a pair of glasses next to the couch. It's as if they're waiting for Kerry to come back and pick up where he left off.

Where the Georgetown home is all crown molding, grand chandeliers, and screams old money, this place is rich colors and inviting plush fabrics.

"How long has it been since you've been here?" I lay a hand on Darren's shoulder to bring his attention back to me.

He leaves his bag in the entryway as he moves forward, running a hand through his hair.

"Years." He flinches slightly at the admission, his voice thick with guilt.

I follow Darren through open living area that leads to the back patio where he slides open the glass door, letting in the cool crisp air that smells like pine, and carries with it the hint of winter. The large deck looks out to a clearing, and in the distance is a pier.

"He closed everything up for the winter," Darren sighs with a disappointed tone. I gather that's something he wasn't expecting.

There are no sounds of traffic, only the occasional rustle of trees and birdsong in the distance, as if we're tucked away from the rest of the world.

Darren stands in the middle of the manicured lawn with the backdrop of grand pines behind him, and his eyes are trained on me, the hint of something dark and needy that sets my pulse racing. I'm imaging him cutting wood and doing outdoorsy things with humor,

He crosses his arms over his chest, stretching the stylish jacket across his chest.

"What's so funny?" he demands.

"I was just picturing you chopping wood in a flannel," I laugh.

"And you find that funny?"

I nod.

"I'll have you know," Darren wiggles his finger in the air, "that I have, in fact, chopped wood before."

I place my hands on my hips and stare at him disbelievingly.

After a moment, Darren concedes. "I didn't say I was good at it," he smiles.

"Does this mean once the wood runs out, we're going to freeze to death?" I question, pointing to the pile by the side of the house.

"Of course not." Darren rolls his eyes. "The house has a heater."

The seriousness with which he says it has me giggling, and Darren grabs hold of me. My stomach twists into knots like the remnants of wisteria that travel along the forest bed and make their way up the sides of the trees, their progress suspended by the impending winter.

"If you want me to wear a flannel," he smiles, tightening his arm around my waist, "I will."

Darren stares down at me, his eyes full of mischief, almost willing me to make another smartass comment, and I'm only too happy to oblige.

"Then you'll have to give me the keys to the car," I explain, and Darren raises both eyebrows in question. "In case you chop off a finger and I have to drive you to the hospital." I can't keep the laughter down that keeps bubbling up inside of me.

Darren gives me a shake and I squeal in response.

"You think you're funny," he entreats.

"Yes," I giggle.

"I'm not going to chop wood in my flannel, Evangeline." He peers down at me in such a way that causes my heart to race. I tilt my head, waiting for what he's going to say next. "I'm going to wear it while I fuck you in every room of this house." He reaches down and hauls me over his shoulder.

"Darren!" I squeal, while he carries me like a lumberjack into the house, smacking my ass on the way.

14

Being a Liberal Would Have Been The Worst

Darren

Taking a walk along the trail through the woods behind the house seemed like a good idea, but it doesn't stop me from thinking how my parents had closed everything up for the winter before they left – before that fateful helicopter flight. It's not just the boat or the cut firewood, but even the pipes outside the house have been covered to prevent freezing. Those are tasks I used to help my father with when I was younger, and although it's been years since I've been here, and countless times I didn't help him, this time feels worse.

I don't regret coming here, but I didn't know how it would make me feel until I did.

"You're quiet," Evangeline says while rubbing her hands together to warm them.

"I was just thinking about how I used to help my dad," I admit, shoving my hands in my pockets.

The thick trees block out most of the sun, making it feel colder than it actually ,is but I wanted to show Evangeline the trail in case she wanted to go for a run during our visit. I plan on celebrating Thanksgiving here and to pack a few things of my parents before heading back to Georgetown.

"Is that something you did often?" she asks.

"Around this time every year, but I stopped coming when I started law school." I kick at the dirt with the toe of my shoe making an indent through the pine needles. "It was my way of punishing him for making me go in the first place."

"But you liked law school."

I shrug. "Yeah, but I was a shit and would never admit that to him."

She loops her arm through mine as we continue down the path. "He might have already known."

"You're probably right. I used to like helping him, so I was only punishing myself really. I think it was the monotony of the task and the quietness in which we did it that made me feel close to him."

The trail meanders along the lake, and the trees finally open up letting in the sun and raising the temperature, although I kind of like Evangeline huddled up close to me.

"When we were busy pulling in the boat or covering the windows, it seemed as though he wasn't worried about what I was going to do with my life, and in turn I didn't have to pretend to care."

"Surely there were other things you could talk about, things you had in common," she prods.

"There was more than just my future we disagreed on." I count on my fingers. "Healthcare reform, student debt, taxes. The worst was my stance on gun control, even though my father was an NRA card carrying Republican," I laugh.

"The shame you must have brought on your family for being a liberal," she jokes.

I can't help but laugh. "I've done some pretty questionable things, but being a liberal would have been the worst."

"What? I'm scandalized," Evangeline teases, pressing a hand to her heart, and I knock into her playfully.

"My mother came from a long line of Republicans. Her father would have disowned her if she married a liberal," I explain lightheartedly. "It was bad enough that my father didn't come from a prominent family."

"Ah, so that's where you get your pretentiousness from," she taunts with amusement in her tone.

"Just remember, only half of my DNA comes from my father, so I'm only half as pretentious," I jest but we both go silent, and I think it's the mention of my father in that way – that there is a part of him in me, perhaps the part that she was so enamored with all those years ago. Maybe there is hope for me yet.

"I take it tradition is a big deal in your family?"

"My life was mapped out for me before I was born because *of* tradition. I may have been at odds with my father over it, but it started generations ago on my mother's side."

"I thought you had a close relationship with your mother?"

"Yes, but I'm not ignorant about what old money means, and what being on the wrong side of history looks like."

She lets out a heavy sigh. "No one ever expected anything of me, except for my grandmother," she clears her throat. "Putting her in a care home was the hardest decision I ever had to make, and I've felt guilty about it every day since, even though it was the right thing to do." She looks down at her feet as she steps over an exposed root on the trail. "I hated leaving her there, especially when she didn't understand why she couldn't stay in her own home anymore."

"You love your grandmother."

"Very much."

"And she's the reason you needed the money."

She stops walking but she doesn't look at me, she just stares at the lake, and I regret bringing it up until she turns and looks at me. She's full of layers, and I'm just now understanding what has been underneath all this time.

"Darren..." She lifts her arms as if she wants to protest but then lowers them.

"You don't have to tell me if you don't want to."

"Are you telling me you don't already know?" she speculates, and that heavy feeling in my chest is back, pressing hard against my heart.

"I guess that's fair," I concede, "but it wasn't personal."

"It is personal – just not to you." She shakes her head. "I was a college student who couldn't keep my scholarship because I was too overwhelmed with personal shit at home and just trying to keep my head above water." Her eyes swim with emotion, and I want more than anything to eviscerate whatever pain she had to go through because it tears me up inside, and I don't care what that says about me.

"And then I met your father, and I just," she pauses, looking at me as if she wants to make sure I can handle hearing this. "I just needed something more, something to hold onto."

She wipes a tear from her cheek and turns away from me.

"My grandmother ran out of money, and I couldn't afford to pay for her healthcare. I had an opportunity to make a lot of money, and I took it."

"You make it sound like it was nothing."

"It was *not* nothing, Darren, but I made peace with it a long time ago."

The silence between us feels fragile, and not even the trees want to risk breaking it as the leaves rustle timidly among the branches. Evangeline shoves her hands back in her pockets, and continues to walk the path, as if signifying the conversation is closed. When I catch up, I touch her arm to stop her. She turns to me and the wind picks up, causing ripples in the once-stoic lake which mimic the changing shades of blue in her eyes as she stares back at me.

It's the tightness in my chest and something deep and dark within my belly that whispers *like calls to like*, because

Evangeline and I – dare I say it – are the same. Maybe I knew this all along. Maybe I knew it the minute she looked at me in the alley of the bar and that's why I couldn't let her walk away, just like I can't let her walk away now.

"I'm sorry."

"Oh, Darren," she glowers and walks away. I catch up, holding onto her arm to stop her again.

"I didn't say it to anger you."

"What do you want me to say? That it's okay because you didn't know that you took away my only means to help my grandmother?" She doesn't know how much her words affect me; how much it eats away at me.

"There are a lot of things I wish I'd done differently."

"You and me both," she sighs.

"What was it about him?" I dare to ask.

"Darren," she warns, and I can see the turmoil in her eyes.

There's a part of me that's desperate to know, and a part of me that should just let it go.

"You said you went to his lecture. What was it about him that stayed with you all this time?" I probe, because I've never been good at letting things lay. "I was his son, and I didn't get that part of him – you did."

Her expression softens as if she can tell how much this means to me.

"I need this Evan," I plead.

She furrows her brows. "What if I can't give you what you need?

"Trust me that whatever you tell me, I'll make peace with it."

15
What Does Emerson Have To Do With Politics?
FOUR YEARS EARLIER

Evangeline

he lecture hall is half-filled, and I find a strategic spot in the back because yet again, I'm late. I didn't get to hear the introduction but find myself instantly enthralled as Senator Walker stands on the stage, addressing our student senate and potential law students.

"I know you've probably got a hundred lawyer jokes brewing in your heads right now, and perhaps you'll stick around after and I'll let you know if I've heard them before," Kerry says, and the room erupts into genuine laughter.

He looks so comfortable up at the podium, with his easy smile and full lips as his hands grip the edges. He's wearing the same suit as this morning when I'd run into him – a crisp dark blue jacket, with a light blue shirt, and a striped tie.

While he tells the students about his law career, he walks away from the podium, holding the mic in hand as he casually moves around the stage as if he's taking a stroll. For someone who is much older than me, his broad shoulders and lean waist make him seem younger, fit for his age – quite handsome. I'm not the only one in the room who thinks so, judging by the ration of female-to-male student body.

"When you stand up and take your oath," he holds his hand in the air, "I will conduct myself uprightly, and according to the law, and I will support the Constitution of the United States," he recites with a passionate yet commanding tone. *"Support the Constitution of the United States,"* he repeats, distinguishing each word to signify their importance, while walking the stage, and it's so quiet and cavernous that I can hear my own breath and feel my heart-beat against my ribs.

"What a monumental burden that is," he asserts. "And it is a burden, the single most important piece of history there is, and the weight of it you will carry around for the rest of your career," he explains.

"Virtue," he pauses as if he's searching inside himself, pulling at little pieces of his heart for inspiration. He looks out at the students, who are sitting at the edges of their seats, waiting to hear what he has to say next. "When the Muses nine/With the Virtues meet/Find to their design/An Atlantic seat/By green orchard boughs. Fended from the heat/Where the statesman ploughs," he recites an Emerson poem, and I wonder if anyone else in the room recognizes it.

I think I'm invisible, but he meets my eyes just before he finishes the rest of the poem. I'm unable to look away. From this distance, I wouldn't be able to make out their color, but I know they're a sunburst mixture of greens, browns, and gold that were made further unearthly by the intensity of the Arizona sun.

"Furrow for the *wheat*/When the Church is social worth/When the statehouse is the hearth/Then the perfect State is come/The republican at home." He pauses, letting his hand drop to his side, the mic along with it, as if to let those words settle in, burrow themselves into the minds of the students whose attention he commands.

He brings the mic back up to his lips. Before he speaks again, he runs his fingers over his jaw. "Emerson," he states, "believed in an ideal government, and to protect individuals' rights."

He looks around the room, finding me once more.

"You might wonder, what the hell does Emerson have to do with politics?" He gives me a secret smile. I know he's speaking to me.

"Everything." He pauses, and the auditorium bubbles with chatter.

Kerry motions with his hand for everyone to quiet down further until there's only a few whispers.

"And if I had the time, I would explain it to you, but they've only allowed me an hour before I get the hook." He motions as if an imaginary hook is pulling him off the stage, causing the students to laugh. "Now, I know I've talked for way too long and I appreciate the time you've allowed for me to hopefully inspire and give you some insight into the path you've chosen, or the one you're still undecided on, but if there is anything I want you to remember from today it is this – the only person you are destined to become is the person you decide to be."

The room dissolves into applause, students stand, some making their way out of the lecture hall, and others milling about the front of the stage. I watch as he greets eager students, shakes their hands, and even graciously signs text-books, or whatever is on hand, as if he's some kind of rockstar.

I stay longer than necessary, stuck between the awkward-ness of making my presence known, and standing in line like an eager groupie.

When the last of the students make their way out of the lecture hall, I make my way to the front of the stage, stepping quietly and feeling a bit like a skittish deer. While shaking the hand of who I presume to be one of the university administrators, he meets my eyes and greets me with a warm smile that instantly puts me at ease.

"No coffee this time," I reassure, holding my hands up as if to show him I'm unarmed, "so you're safe."

He turns his attention fully on me and it's like being swallowed up in the ocean. "Well, if it isn't the white rabbit," he entreats teasingly, and in those few words is an imperceptible hint of a southern drawl that he seemed so carefully to hide during his speech.

"This time I'm not running late," I laugh nervously.

I stand there, not sure what to say next, and not really knowing why I'm here anyway. I say the only thing I can think of. "Evangeline." I hold my hand out to officially meet him. He smiles broadly and takes hold of my hand. It's warm and soft, and the minute our palms connect, it feels as though I've stepped through the looking glass.

"It's nice to meet you, Evangeline." He gives me a slight wink as if it's an inside secret, because the only other person who knows we met before is his security detail.

Suddenly, I'm aware that there are only a handful of people left in the lecture hall.

An older gentleman with bright blue eyes and a nice smile approaches us. "Great speech," he declares, and Kerry turns, giving the man his full attention. "But I'm afraid those kids are more inspired by some celebrity than Emerson." The man laughs, clapping Kerry's shoulder in a friendly gesture.

"That's not true," Kerry disagrees, and then turns toward me as I stand awkwardly, formulating a way to leave without bringing more attention to myself. "Evangeline here is a scholar of Emerson," he gushes, and then everyone's attention causes my cheeks to heat.

"Is that so?" the man inquires, and intuitively Kerry takes charge of the conversation as if he knows how uncomfortable I am with the attention.

"Not all of today's youth are preoccupied with technology

and celebrity. There are those bright few who find solace in the pages of history, the birth of our country, and the hopes that were bled into those pages," he effuses, and when he looks at me, it's as if he can see inside to a memory of me in the library, pressing an open book to my nose, feeling the pages, and reading them like I wanted to jump inside.

It's arresting how much his attention affects me, like I'm starved for it.

"What is it about Emerson that you find so appealing?" the man asks.

Before I can answer, a woman interrupts. "Sir, we need to leave in order to make our reservation," she explains.

Kerry nods, and I try hard to school my expression. I'll never get the chance to tell him how much his speech moved me, fueled something in me on a day that seemed impossible, a day I thought would be the pebble that would cause everything to topple over.

I watch as Kerry shakes a few hands, gives them an effortless politician's smile before he turns back to me.

"I'd love it if you would indulge us in a conversation about Emerson," he pauses, looking at his friend, "and insights into today's youth," he adds. "I'd like to prove to my friend here that your generation is not only interested in celebrity," he teases.

"Always the politician," his friend says, a ruddy smile on his face. He then turns to me. "Yes, please," he grins. "I'd love to hear what you'd have to say about what issues your demographic faces," he explains.

Demographic? I'm twenty, and I didn't even register until this past year, not even in time to vote in this year's primaries. I mean to say no, I *should* say no, but then Kerry smiles, showing his bright white teeth and it travels into his eyes, glinting off the harsh fluorescent lights of the lecture hall.

"I think we'd all be interested in what you have to say," Kerry encourages.

I nod, flushing slightly and then realize I'm wearing tight faded jeans and a light pink shirt that I picked up a long time ago at a thrift shop near school.

Kerry smiles, noticing that I'm looking down at my clothes. "Your attire is fine for the restaurant we're eating at," he reassures me.

As if he's already anticipating the thoughts running through my head about not having enough money in my bank account to even buy a value meal at a fast-food restaurant, he adds, "Dinner is on me." He gives me that imperceptible wink again that floods my cheeks with heat.

"Thanks," I beam and then he turns his attention back to the woman, has a conversation I can't hear, but she leaves, walking ahead of us.

"So, Miss...?" His friend smiles at me, urging me forward.

"Bowen," I say.

"Miss Bowen," he says and holds out his hand.

"Jonathan Langley," he introduces himself. "Senator Jonathan Langley," he clarifies.

I find myself in a very low-key pizza joint near campus that I had passed by many times. It's not a place I ever thought a congressman would eat, but Kerry looks right at home except for his expensive looking suit looking out of place at the worn wooden bench table covered by a plastic plaid tablecloth. At the center are two large pizzas, still steaming from the brick oven.

Kerry sits on the opposite side of the table from me, and I laugh when he tucks a napkin into the collar of his dress shirt before taking a bite of pizza. Mary, his aide, as I learned on the way over, stands and directs a gentleman with a camera to take pictures. Kerry smiles, and the minute the flashes stop,

I notice the look he gives Mary, his brows furrowed, and shakes his head.

She seems to understand his meaning and stops the pictures, taking the man out of the restaurant, only to return alone a few minutes later.

The conversation is light, not at all what I expected, and I'm put at ease, giving practiced answers about my major and background.

"I bet your parents are proud," Mary exclaims next to me after I had explained that I got into college on partial scholarships.

I don't have many people asking about my background or my family, but I've already developed canned answers; little white lies that don't hurt anyone but me. I certainly don't want to explain to anyone that my father died before I even knew who he was. I wouldn't tell them how the man my mother married looked at me with something in his eyes that made my stomach turn.

"Yes, they are," I agree, giving my own politician's smile as I take a bite of pizza.

"And a literature major too. Are you as big a fan of Emerson as Senator Walker?" she asks.

"I'd like to say that my professors share the same enthusiasm as Senator Walker, but they make reading him and other nineteenth century poetry feel like a chore," I admit.

"What a shame," Kerry exhales. "Do the other students share your same sentiment?" he asks, taking a sip of his dark ale.

I think about that for a moment, remembering the sounds of pages turning, fingers tapping against keyboards, Professor Abbot's monotone voice, and how there never seems to be lively debates. "I think they just want to make it to the end of the semester with a passing grade," I answer honestly.

"And you?" he inquires, and the question is so wide and

vast it threatens to fill my lungs with so much potential that they will burst.

"I want to be inspired," I blurt, and it feels like I'm giving away a part of myself, something I don't give to anyone, because no one had ever asked.

"And were you inspired today?" he challenges, and perhaps I'm the only one who notices, but the golds and greens of his eyes are hungry for my answer, eager for me to admit that I was indeed inspired because it would please him.

"Yes," I answer honestly, and I'm rewarded with a bashful smile; a pleased smile.

"I think you have a fan," Senator Langley notices, and I quickly school my expression.

"If you were the literature teacher, it would be the most popular class on campus," I insist.

Senator Langley laughs, clapping Kerry's shoulder just like he did earlier. "If politics doesn't work out, you seem to have a teaching career in your future." The table erupts into easy laughter, and whatever anxiety I had felt earlier about whether I belonged here or not is ebbed away by it. It's not often I have a table full of powerful men eager to hear what I have to say. I quite like it. It's fueling something inside of me to want more out of life.

"So tell me, what issues does your demographic face these days?" Senator Walker queries.

I sit up a little straighter, my confidence having been stoked by their attentiveness.

"I don't think I'm the average college student you expected," I offer, "other than having to worry about student debt, I'm a twenty-year-old female who struggles to pay for college, and an ailing grandmother with expensive prescription medications, not to mention elderly care – *good* elderly care – is astronomical."

Kerry clears his throat. "Mary, did you get all that?" he

asks, and Mary hurriedly pulls out her notepad, writing things down.

"You don't have to…"

"I asked because I wanted to know."

I nod.

Kerry sets down his pizza, wiping his mouth with his napkin. "Well, this is uh," he pauses as if searching for the right words.

"Not very good pizza?" I offer, because Arizona is not known for great pizza.

Kerry laughs. "No, it's not."

"You should have asked me and I would have directed you to the best taco stand in town," I tease.

"Well, I'll have to remember for next time." He pushes his plate away and then takes a sip of his beer.

Next time? Does he plan on coming back? I can't help that the thought of it causes a thrill to run through me.

I don't know much about politics, but I wonder why a Senator from Virginia would be visiting an Arizona University.

Is he positioning himself to run for President?

My attention is pulled away from my inner thoughts when I hear Senator Langley ask Kerry, "How is it you know Miss Bowen again?"

He offers an answer that I didn't expect, and it comes out so effortlessly that it doesn't feel like a lie, and even though I know it is, it feels like the truth.

"She's a friend of my son Darren's," he explains without missing a beat, and I can feel something in the pit of my stomach, something wrong and hollow, but when I look up, I can see the regret in his eyes. Kerry is a Senator and I'm a student; more importantly, I'm a young, *female* student. There can't be any misunderstanding. No matter how innocently we met, it would seem odd that he would invite me to dinner if he didn't previously know me.

Senator Langley looks at me expectantly as if I'm supposed to elaborate, but my mouth is clamped shut.

"Well, hopefully she influences him to carry your torch for Emerson," Senator Langley laughs, holding out his hand to me. "It was lovely meeting you Miss Bowen." He smiles, kissing my knuckles, and even though it's a polite gesture, there's something behind his smile that doesn't feel right. He releases me and says his goodbyes while I gather my things.

We linger on the sidewalk; Mary, Senator Walker, and his security man that waits by a black sedan at the curb.

"I'll be a few minutes, Bailey," Kerry says, and Bailey steps away to stand near the car.

Mary excuses herself, telling me how wonderful it was to meet me in such a genuine way that she leaves me blushing. She doesn't get into the black sedan ,but another car I didn't notice parked behind it. I am fully aware that it's just Kerry and I on the street, the spring Arizona heat curling the hairs on the back of my neck.

"Thank you for indulging me this evening. You made this old man feel important," he says kindly.

"You made *me* feel important, like my opinion mattered."

"It does matter," he consoles with sincerity.

"And you're not that old," I add, even though it is true he could be my father, he doesn't act like a father, or at least none that I know. But the word *old* puts a line between us, one that I want to step over – one that I *ache* to step over, ignoring the fact that the gold wedding band on his left hand reflects the light from a nearby streetlamp.

He reaches out, taking a piece of my hair between his fingers, and I shiver as if the strands of my hair have nerve endings, and I can feel it the same as if he were touching my skin.

Tilting his head, he looks at me thoughtfully, and I know what he's going to say before he says it. Embarrassment unfurls in my stomach, turning to sadness.

"You know I can't ask you to come back to my hotel room with me, right?" he implies, his voice laced with regret, and dare I say with a hint of the same longing I feel.

I nod, unable to trust my voice, and I feel something claw its way up my throat threatening to make its way out, something like a whine or a protest, but I know better.

"You are a very bright young woman, and you should remember that," he insists.

I ask myself why I'm so enamored by this man that I only met today, how I feel connected to him, but the answer eludes me.

"You have to know how inspired I was today – especially today – when I needed it most," I admit.

He lets go of my hair and it's as if he's released me, his words bringing me back. "You have renewed my faith in the young people of today, Miss Bowen."

The space between us is charged like the air right before a storm, full of untapped energy just waiting to be ignited.

"My angel – his name is Freedom/Choose him to be your king/He shall cut pathways east and west/And fend you with his wing."

"The Boston Hymn's fourth stanza," I observed, quietly.

"Do you know what it means?" he inquires, and I shake my head.

"It means to elect freedom as king. God's own angel, sent to rebuke the misdeeds who sit on the throne and replace them with freedom, and he will protect you with his wing."

I'm not sure I understand it, but I take the morsel and stuff it in my pocket for safe keeping.

"Thank you," I manage to say.

He smiles, and a soft laugh escapes his lips. "For what?"

"For renewing my faith in Emerson," I confirm.

"Ah," he graces me with a mysterious smile. "You were always faithful. Perhaps you just needed a reminder."

16

Respectable Gentlemen
Darren

"*I*'m not that naïve girl anymore. I understand the difference now between someone being nice and when there's real interest there. Your father..." she falters, and I stay quiet, holding my breath as I give her time to finish.

"He saw in me something that I needed, something I was desperate for." She shrugs. "There wasn't anything inappropriate, Darren."

"Maybe I wanted to see something bad in him," I admit. "Because if there was a fault, I could justify my anger."

It's not just my anger at the situation, it was my anger with him by creating this shadow that was impossible to step out from.

"But that's the thing. We all have faults. Perhaps he didn't spend enough time at home, put work first, didn't go to your little league games, or expected too much from you. Those are his faults. Being unfaithful wasn't one of them."

I shrug and turn away from her, looking out at the woods.

"I wasted so much time being angry, when he's not the one I should have been angry with."

I run a hand over my jaw and feel Evangeline touch my shoulder.

"I wish I had known you," I say, turning around to face her.

"Don't be angry at your father for lying to Langley that you're how we knew each other. You know why he did it."

"I'm not, I just wish I did know you, because maybe…"

"I think we both know you're no knight in shining armor," she teases.

I chuckle and raise an eyebrow. "You're right about that. I just sometimes wish I could be that person."

"What kind of person?" She furrows her brows.

"The one that saves someone instead of having to *be* saved."

"I don't need saving, Darren," she protests. "I made a choice to do what I did for a living, and if I had to make it all over again, I would, because that's what you do for the people you love."

I place a hand to her cheek and feel how cold it is. "I have never wanted to be the kind of person people look up to, but you," I brush my thumb along her lower lip, "make me *ache* to start."

"So, what are you going to do about that?" she challenged.

"I don't know." I scratch the back of my neck. "I only know what I haven't done about it, and I can't watch while everyone else's life moves on. Even Alistair has a fucking job," I scoff.

"I know what that's like," she offers.

"When we were viewing the Declaration of Inde-pendence…"

"Is that what you call it?" she teases, her cheeks turning a lovely shade of pink.

I laugh a little bashfully. "You said, *this is your Emerson*, and I had never thought of it in that way before."

With those words I had felt seen. I wasn't in the shadow of someone who was larger and greater than me, I had stepped into the light.

"Sometimes we can't see ourselves the way other people can."

"You're a very observant person."

"Occupational hazard," she teases.

"I'm gonna take the Bar in February," I blurt out, like ripping off a Band-Aid, as if it were something to get through rather than savor. "It's barely enough time, and if I want to pass, I'll have to spend all my time studying, but, Evangeline," I pause to take a breath, "I feel really good about this."

"You're going to take the Bar?" she asks in shock.

"Don't look so surprised. I can be a respectable gentleman of society," I tease, but she just narrows her eyes at me seeing right through my bullshit.

"Why now, Darren? What's changed?"

"Everything." I kick at an innocent rock. "Fate and legacy have caught up to me. I can't run anymore." I peer at her, wondering what she's thinking. "What am I going to do with my life? Because this isn't working for me anymore," I gesture to the house. "My parents aren't coming back. It's time I lived up to my potential, to take what's mine."

I take her hand and even through her glove, it burns through me.

"I want more, Evan."

I leave Evangeline asleep in bed to start a pot of coffee. Thank God this house has a regular machine and not one of those fancy ones that only a barista would know how to use.

I woke up feeling better than I had in a decade, like a weight had been lifted off me, even though deciding to take the Bar should be more pressure than I could handle. It's given me something to work towards, and I haven't had that in a long time.

The deceiving blue sky causes me to step onto the deck where I smell the burned notes of a fire from a nearby chimney, along with pine needles and everything that says fall is coming to an end and winter is closing in fast – along with my balls shriveling up and trying to climb back inside my body to get away from the cold.

"Shit!"

It's like participating in the polar plunge where people skinny dip in the middle of winter for reasons I can't fathom. I shiver and curse, trying to think of why I was so stupid to come out here in the first place, when the front door bangs open. I turn around to see Alistair standing in the doorway where he drops his luggage, and his eyes drop to my flaccid cock.

"Well," he heckles, pointing at me. "It doesn't look like you're happy to see me."

"Jesus *fuck*, Alistair," I move into the kitchen and grab a dish towel to cover myself. "I was just outside and it's fucking cold."

"Why are you here so early anyway? I said to come the day before Thanksgiving."

"Have you been so busy fucking Evangeline – poor thing – to know what day it is?" He makes a *tsk* noise while trying to peer over the counter as I wave him away angrily. It dawns on me, today *is* the day before Thanksgiving. I palm my face, nearly dropping the towel.

Evangeline appears from the hallway with sleepy eyes, dressed in the long underwear that we picked up in town.

"Did I interrupt something?" she muses, looking at the dishtowel I'm holding in front of me and back at Alistair.

"No. *Jesus*," I grumble.

From behind Alistair, Cleo appears, her leopard print bag hanging at her side. "Darren, now I know you didn't invite me here for an orgy." Her other hand is at her waist. "That costs extra," she snickers with a wink.

"Oh my God!" Evangeline runs towards her. "What are you doing here?"

The timing may not be optimal, but the look on Evangeline's face is worth standing here with a flaccid cock that may or may not have frostbite.

17
Where's The Turkey?
Evangeline

"What do you mean we're not having Thanksgiving dinner?" Alistair bellows in outrage. "Where's the turkey? The sweet potatoes?"

Darren forgot to put in the order, and in this small town, no restaurants are open.

He holds up a silencing finger with the phone pressed to his ear. "I don't think you understand. I can pay you *anything*," Darren insists to the person on the other end. "Yes, I realize you're not a magician and can't make a turkey appear out of thin air." He looks over at me rolling his eyes, but I can't help finding the humor in the situation. "Can you call other grocers and find a turkey?" Darren demands, changing focus. He drops his head and pinches his forehead. "No, I don't think you're a turkey concierge."

"Is there such a thing as a turkey concierge?" he whispers to me, and I shake my head.

Cleo's shoulders shake with laughter, and I can't help but join her.

"Why didn't you just cook a turkey?" Alistair directs his question at me.

Cleo puts a hand on her hip, pressing her lips together and fighting to keep her words in.

"Does having ovaries automatically make me a Michelin chef?" I question, offended.

Alistair, seeing the error of his ways, shuts his mouth while Darren laughs, shoving his phone in his back pocket with a defeated huff.

"Trust me, even eggs and bacon are a stretch." I open my mouth to protest, but he silences me by saying, "And before you get offended, I can barely use the espresso machine, so neither of us are in a position to cook a full-on turkey dinner, even if I were to go out in the woods and shoot one," Darren consoles.

Alistair begins to laugh; first a chortle, and then a full-on attack. He barely gets the words out when he says, "Are you fucking Davy Crockett?"

"No, Alistair. I am not!" Darren curls his fingers into his palm, and I can see the situation escalating so I step in.

"I might have a solution."

A few searches on my phone, one call which was received enthusiastically, a twenty-minute drive later, and we're standing outside of the Living Word Ministries.

"I think you planned this," Cleo accuses.

"It's a Methodist church, it would be like cheating on the Catholic. They can smell guilt like a bloodhound, ya know," Alistair declares to Darren.

"Quit making excuses. I would worry less about what your Catholic brethren think and more about your waiter skills." I raise an eyebrow.

"Darren," Alistair whines, ignoring me. "I gave up Caroline and Remington's *actual* Michelin chef thanksgiving dinner for this." He peers up at the welcome sign that says *Feed your faith, and your fears will starve to death.* He points dramatically at the red brick building.

Darren is staring at me with a smile, his eyes alight with that ever-present mischief, but now there's something deeper within the hazel swirls. Even though he may have been hesitant about coming here in the beginning, I can feel that hesitation start to ebb away.

Cleo clears her throat breaking the spell. "Kinda cold out here." She pulls me forward, her ankle length leopard print fur coat flapping against my leg.

From behind, I hear Darren chastising Alistair, "If I hear one more complaint, I'm gonna throw you in the lake when we get back to the house."

Inside, the dining hall is decorated with turkey printed table cloths and filled with people. Through the crowd, I notice a young woman with gloves wearing a hair net making rounds refilling cups with a different variety of drinks. I catch her eye and she makes her way over.

"I'm Evangeline. I called earlier," I explain.

"Oh yes!" she exclaims excitedly. "I'm Maria. Thank you so much. We're short on volunteers and could really use the help," she says breathlessly, balancing a tray of drinks.

"You can put your coats over there." She points to a small room off the kitchen and then assesses the four of us. "You," she points to Alistair, "you look strong."

"Well, I mean looks… looks can be deceiving," Alistair stutters.

"Here," she hands him the tray. "Just refill drinks, there's iced tea, lemonade, and water, and you can grab more in the kitchen if you run out."

Alistair balances the tray and wobbles over to a nearby table, looking back at us with a distressed look.

"I could use some hands filling up plates," she orders, pointing to me and Darren, and motions for us to follow her to the line of guests at a buffet style table.

"Why do I feel like the last kid picked for basketball?" Cleo steps forward, placing a hand on her hip.

"Do you have any experience prepping food?" Maria questions.

She inspects her long fingernails before answering. "No time like the present." We all follow Maria into the kitchen where she hands us each a plastic hair net and gloves.

"Do I really have to wear this?" Darren bemoans, holding the plastic cap with disdain.

I grab it from him and snap it on his head. "Picture perfect," I declare, holding out my hands to frame his face.

"You are loving this aren't you?" he grouses while his hands wrap around my waist and he stares down at me, his eyes dropping to my lips. Instead of kissing me, he grabs the plastic cap and shoves it on my head, pulling it over my eyes.

"Hey!" I pull away, adjusting the cap and tucking a few stray hairs in.

Alistair passes by. "If you want to switch, the answer is hell to the no," he laughs and then stops at a nearby table. "Iced tea, lemonade, water?" he asks as if he's a nineteen fifties cigarette girl in a speakeasy.

"Aren't you a cute one," one of the elderly women at the table says to Alistair.

I hear a troubled squeak from him. "Keep your hands to yourself!"

There's a line of people extending outside the door, and I hand Darren a large spoon for the green beans and grab one of my own. We get right to work scooping vegetables, potatoes, and gravy, onto countless plates.

"You look familiar," one of the men says to Darren.

"I have one of those faces," he smiles, but I can tell it makes him uncomfortable.

The man moves along, and I glance behind me to see Cleo in the kitchen placing more cuts of turkey into large aluminum pans, her dark curls barely contained in the plastic cap. She peers over at me, posing with her gloved hands, one sharp nail poking through the plastic. She looks so out of place, but I love it. In fact, I love that we're all here, because this is the first holiday I haven't felt alone.

I still can't believe Darren arranged for Cleo to be here, and even though his intention was to have us all at the lake house sitting at a gorgeously decorated table eating a turkey dinner already prepared, with all the sides and desserts, I think it turned out exactly how it was meant to.

Darren's hand rests on the small of my back and he leans over to absently place a kiss to the side of my head. When he does, Cleo gives me a worried look, and I turn away, concentrating on my task.

I'm a runner, and yet standing on my feet for hours is wearing on me. When Maria closes the doors after the last of the people leave with their bellies full, I pull the cap off my head and swipe at the little beads of sweat that have accumulated.

Alistair places the tray down on a nearby table, and Cleo joins us, releasing her curls from the cap.

"I think I might have a career as a waiter," Alistair declares proudly.

"Hungry?" Maria asks, and I realize that I haven't eaten all day. In fact, none of us have. My stomach grumbles and I look over at Darren who is nodding enthusiastically.

Maria laughs, pointing towards an empty table. "Grab a plate," she announces, and we do, loading them with the leftover turkey, mashed potatoes, and vegetables. Burke, the kitchen chef, places a bowl full of rolls and a tray of butter between us, and then he joins Maria on the other side of the table, along with a couple of the other volunteers.

Alistair picks at his plate, gravy seeping off his turkey and into his vegetables. I watch as his hunger gets the better of him and he reluctantly scoops a forkful, closing his eyes as he puts it in his mouth and chews.

"I can't tell you how much we appreciate your help today. It's always hard getting volunteers on Thanksgiving," Maria explains.

"You can thank Darren for that. He forgot to order our food so that's how we ended up here," I confess.

Darren grumbles something incoherent while chewing on a piece of turkey.

"So, you just came for a free meal then?" Maria teases.

"Hey, I worked for this meal," Alistair states, scooping up another forkful of mashed potatoes.

"Whatever the reason, we're glad to have you."

"How do you fund this place?" Darren probes out of the blue.

"We get by on donations and some grants. You look like you could stand to lose some change from your pocket." Marie points to Darren's designer shirt and jeans that probably cost the same as Alistair's Louboutins.

He laughs and points back at Maria. "You remind me of someone," he jokes, sliding his eyes to me, an amused expression on his face. I know exactly who he's thinking of.

"Someone who kicks ass at getting donations?"

"I'll send a check tomorrow."

"Told you I kicked ass," Maria boasts, pleased with herself.

"Well, I for one, am going to add this to my resume," Alistair pipes up.

"Along with drag queen," Darren adds jokingly.

"Am I ever going to live that down?" Alistair playfully bangs his fist on the table rattling the silverware.

"Not until you fess up on how you ended up in the slammer," Darren counters.

"I feel like I'm missing something," Cleo pipes up.

"I second that," Maria agrees.

"It's nothing," Alistair protests.

"I disagree," Darren counters, turning towards Alistair with raised brows.

"Can we just leave it at hazing?" Alistair demands.

"I'm gonna need context." Cleo peers at both Darren and me for confirmation.

"We had to pick Alistair up at the park police station," I explain.

"I'm still not getting why this is news." She eyes Alistair as if she's already got him pegged.

"He was wearing a dress and heels," I pause, trying to contain my laughter. "They were Louboutins," I clarify.

"A man with good taste." Cleo winks at him.

"See?" Alistair waves his hand to Cleo. "She gets it."

"I'm guessing you're not from here, but there's been a rise in public indecency arrests in the parks," Burke interjects, shoving a forkful of turkey in his mouth as we all stare at him. "Did I not mention that I'm a police officer?"

"Your dress was a little indecent. I'm pretty sure I saw some nip," Darren laughs.

Alistair threatens to fling a forkful of gravy laden green beans at him and I can't contain my laughter.

"Just tell the story!" Cleo demands.

Alistair sets his fork down and flattens out his shirt as if to prepare himself to regale his tales of woe.

"This stays between us," he insists dramatically while looking around the table.

"And the D.C. park police," Darren interjects, to which Alistair rolls his eyes.

"I might have taken a little…" he stops mid-sentence and looks questioningly at Burke who tilts his head.

"I'm off duty," Burke explains, "and frankly, I don't care," he adds, shoveling pumpkin pie into his mouth.

"I might have taken a little ecstasy," he demonstrates the

size by using his pointer finger and thumb, and then turns to Darren. "You know how X makes me *amorous*."

Cleo raises her eyebrows.

"No, I do *not*," Darren protests, appalled.

"Anyway, I obviously couldn't drive myself home, so my work *friends…*"

"I thought we had this conversation about friends," Darren interrupts.

"Can I just finish?" Alistair begs, annoyed.

Darren motions for him to continue.

"They put me in a rideshare, and I guess the woman did not take kindly to my compliments." He shrugs. "To make a long story short…"

"Too late," Burke pipes up and Alistair glares at him.

"She pulls over at the park and tells me to get out. Can you imagine the nerve?"

"She could sue you for sexual harassment," Darren points out.

"Well, look who's not a lawyer but thinks he knows everything." Alistair shakes his head.

"I graduated from law school." Darren gestures. "But besides that, I do know everything," he adds smugly.

"These boys are quite entertaining," Cleo says, only to me, and I laugh.

"I had to take a *piss* and the bathrooms were closed," Alistair continues looking pointedly at Darren with obvious annoyance.

"And?" I ask, because at this point now I'm committed to the story. I have to know how it ends.

"I got caught peeing on a tree," Alistair explains sheepishly.

"That's it?" Darren protests.

"Do you know how many times a day I pee on a tree?" Burke mumbles between bites of his pie.

"You're a police officer," Alistair frets, appalled.

"I'm in a patrol car all day. What do you want me to do?" Burke asks, shrugging.

"Pee at a goddamn gas station like a civilized person," Alistair bemoans.

"Have you seen how dirty those are?" Burke levels him with a stare.

"So you got arrested for peeing on a tree?" I speculate, disappointed.

"Well, that's not all of it," he admits a little bashfully. "When he pointed the flashlight at me, I got startled."

"Please do not tell me what I think you're going to tell me," Darren laughs, shaking his head.

"I turned real fast." Alistair looks between Darren and Burke. "You know how it is. Once you start, you can't stop."

"I'm not following," Maria interjects, innocently.

"I peed on a police officer, okay?"

18

This Isn't A Movie
Evangeline

orning light filters into the bedroom from the patio doors because someone forgot to close the blinds. I groan and rest my forearm over my head, and then drop my arm to the side feeling nothing but rumpled sheets and mattress. Flipping over on my side, I realize Darren's not here and I run my fingers over his side of the bed.

I was used to sleeping alone in Georgetown up until recently, and I wonder when I began to get used to this, used to the feel of someone's body next to me, a body to curl against and share heat with... Darren's body. I hear noise from the kitchen and grab my long underwear from the chair before stepping out into the hallway to discover Darren in the kitchen. He's flipping pancakes, and the smell of bacon causes my stomach to grumble.

"Where were these skills yesterday?" I ask while he slides a pancake from the pan and onto a plate.

"Ask that after you take a bite," he teases, holding out a forkful that he just dipped into syrup.

I take a skeptical bite, trusting the syrup will cover up anything horrible.

"It's not the best pancake I've ever had, but I'm not wanting to spit it out either," I heckle.

"I worked really hard on this." He drops the spatula and turns off the burner.

I walk into his chest as he wraps his arms around me. "I said I didn't want to spit it out." I look up at him with a smile while I rest my chin on his chest.

He smiles down at me with his wolfish grin.

"Have you seen Cleo or Alistair yet?"

"Nope, but these ceilings are too high to hit with the end of a broomstick to wake them," Darren laughs.

"I'll go wake up Cleo," I announce, but my hands remain on Darren's shoulders and I don't move. Instead, I stare at his face, a face I once looked at with disdain. All I see is him, the boy that lost his parents, the self-described degenerate son of a U.S. Senator who arranged for my only friend in the world to be with me on Thanksgiving.

I love that he did that – I love...

He smiles, his cheeks pulling up into his eyes, the dimples more prominent now that he'd shaved yesterday, and I run my fingers over them.

"What?" he probes, his smile fading and the dimples receding.

I kiss him. His hand slides to the back of my neck, fingers splayed and moving into my hair. I feel a shiver of desire make its way down my body. If we didn't have guests, I wouldn't pull away, and when I do, he groans in protest.

"I'll make pancakes more often," he brags, with his eyes half closed.

"Thank you," I mention, and he cocks his head. "For bringing Cleo here."

"She did almost hang up on me. I guess she was still

angry," he explains. "But it was nothing that a private plane couldn't cure."

"I think you know the way to Cleo's heart," I tease, placing a hand on his chest. "But seriously, I'm just… I can't believe you did that."

Darren pierces me with those complicated eyes of his and gives me an unintentionally wolfish smile. "For you, anything," he murmurs unabashedly, and it sets my pulse racing, causing a knot to form in my stomach.

I pull away. "I should go wake her," I declare, leaving Darren in the kitchen as I run up the stairs that lead to the loft.

When I get to Cleo's room, I hear the creak of a door on the other side open.

I was already prepared with a smart-ass comment about him sleeping in when I turn to see Cleo exiting Alistair's room.

"Uh, you know we're gonna talk about this later, right?"

Cleo waves me off as she passes by and shuts her door. When I look back, I see Alistair poking his head around the door and then he ducks back in.

"Oh, by the way, Darren made pancakes!" I yell to both of them and then head back down the stairs.

"Are they coming?" he asks, unaware of why his question causes fits of giggles.

"Oh, if I know Cleo, I'm sure they both did."

Alistair descends the stairs a few moments later, looking as if nothing is wrong.

"Smells good." He saunters into the kitchen and plucks a piece of bacon from the plate. "What's up?" He casually leans against the counter chewing on his bacon.

"Did you just fuck my friend?" I challenge with narrowed eyes, placing my hand on my hip.

"Yeah." He shrugs looking innocently between Darren and me.

When I catch Darren's eye, he throws his hands up and mouths, *not my problem.*

"What's the big deal?" Alistair asks.

"Because she's my friend!" I whisper shout while pointing up to the loft, just as Cleo makes her way down.

"Wow, if you're this protective over who she fucks, you must be exhausted," he laughs.

"This is not funny." I smack him with a potholder.

"Hey, hey!" Alistair holds his hands up while laughing. "Are you going to let your wife abuse me like this?" Alistair whines, looking to Darren for help.

"You're on your own." Darren stands with his arms crossed over his chest as he watches the scene unfold.

"What's all the fuss about?" Cleo questions, giving Alistair's butt a squeeze when she passes by, causing him to squeal.

I shake my head and laugh, "I think I need some fresh air," I announce, throwing the potholder back onto the counter.

"I'll go with you," Cleo confirms, pouring herself a fresh cup of coffee while I head into the bedroom so I can change and grab a jacket. When I come back out, Cleo is leaning against the kitchen counter, casually laughing at something Darren said. I watch quietly for a moment before Darren notices me and Cleo turns around.

"Ready?" I zip up my jacket.

"You don't want to eat?" Darren holds up a forkful of pancakes while I open the back patio door.

I scrunch up my face. "I'll pass," I apologize, slipping through the doorway and holding it open for Cleo to pass with an amused look on her face.

"More for me!" I hear him yell behind me as Cleo shuts the door.

She's still chuckling as we make our way across the deck and down the stairs to the clearing. The ends of her red scarf flutter in the breeze as we walk towards the dock.

"I didn't fuck him for money." She turns to me with a smile. "Have you seen that cute little ass?" she muses with a wink, and unfortunately, I have. "I gave him a freebie."

I laugh, digging my toe into the ground to push up a weed as I shove my hands in the pockets of my jacket. The morning air is crisp and cuts like a knife, but the sky is a robin's egg blue like that of a sunny summer day.

"I thought he was going to break down and cry yesterday when you told him we were going to go serve food at the church," Cleo laughs.

"I think Alistair is more used to writing checks than refilling drinks," I bemuse. "Although, he did manage to charm that one cranky elderly woman who kept complaining the turkey was dry."

"I wasn't sure about these rich boys at first, but they're growing on me," she offers.

"I'm sure it doesn't have anything to do with the private jet?" I raise an eyebrow.

She uses her fingers to demonstrate. "Just a tiny bit," she laughs and then stops us just before we get to the dock. "I missed you."

Her eyes are like molten pools of brown. I've never known Cleo to get emotional. She's always tough as nails.

"I missed you, too." I give her a hug and squeeze as tight as our bulky jackets will let us. "The year will be over before you know it," I reassure, my voice muffled by her curly hair.

She pulls away, a sad expression on her face. "You won't be back."

I let go of her and continue walking on the dock towards the end.

"I don't know what I'm going to do yet." I shrug, taking a seat in one of the Adirondack chairs.

"No." She places a hand over mine "I mean you won't be

back because that boy in there is in love with you." She points towards the house,

Her bluntness throws me off and causes heat to rush to my cheeks.

"No, he's not. It's just…"

"You might be every boy's wet dream, but I know the difference between pussy whipped and love, hun." She looks at me pointedly.

"This isn't a movie, Cleo," I sigh. "I'm not a prostitute with a heart of gold who gets the billionaire at the end," I add dramatically.

Cleo purses her lips but remains quiet.

I lean further back in my chair, staring at the lake and chewing my fingernail. Cleo might think she knows everything, but she doesn't know Darren, and she doesn't know us. What we've been doing is playing house, and that's not real.

None of this is real.

19

Tread Carefully
Darren

A listair points to the boxes on the floor. "Finally going through your parents' things?" he asks, cautiously.

"Just taking some things back to Georgetown with me."

"You're never going to sell this place, are you?" He looks around the library.

"No."

"So you're really doing it," Alistair comments, lighting up a cigar.

I crack open the patio door of the library letting in the cold November air. "Who are you, Hugh Hefner?"

Alistair crosses an ankle over his knee and puffs on the cigar exaggeratedly.

"Don't deflect. You're studying for the Bar," he points to the textbooks on the desk. "Does this mean you're going to hand over your freedom and join me in wearing a suit and tie?" he challenges, holding the cigar out in front of him to inspect it. "By the way, your father has good taste."

I take a seat behind the desk, running a hand over my face. "Yeah, so?"

"What does that mean?" He takes another puff of the cigar, the smoke billowing around him.

"I don't know what it means. I just know that it's time to quit being angry and do something for myself, and not because I think it will piss off Rausch or my father."

"Spoken like a card-carrying adult," Alistair teases. "But this is big."

"It's time I grow up. My parents aren't coming back and I just… I want more out of life. Even you have a fucking job," I scoff.

"Riding my coattails, Dare?" Alistair teases.

I crumple up a piece of paper on the desk and throw it at him. "Hardly. By the way, Cleo?"

"What can I say? Evangeline has fine friends." He puffs on the cigar while smiling wolfishly as I shake my head.

"Speaking of," Alistair sits up in his chair. "You sent a private jet for her?" he questions, almost offended.

"Nevada is farther away than D.C.," I remind him with an annoyed tone. "Were you expecting your own plane?"

"Of course not," Alistair scoffs. "My point is that a) you brought her here, and b) you sent a private plane."

"Is there some cryptic meaning here that I'm not getting because a) she's Evangeline's friend, and b) it was last minute." I glare at him.

"The point is you seem to be doing a lot of things for Evangeline lately." Alistair takes a puff of the cigar and cocks a skeptical eyebrow.

I gesture for him to continue.

"A little birdie told me you gave her a private viewing of a priceless artifact at the National Archives Museum." He gives me a smug smile and then tries to make a smoke ring.

"If you're referring to the Emerson letters, then I'm guessing Bethany told Caroline and it became dinner gossip at the Van der Walt home?" I speculate, already knowing the answer.

"D.C. is a very small town, Darren."

As if I don't already know that. "I wanted to make up for what I did to get her here," I impart with a shrug.

"Are you sure it's nothing more than your guilty conscience?" Alistair asks, drumming his fingers on the arm of the chair.

"What's that supposed to mean?" I question, with a bit of edge to my tone.

Alistair shrugs, tapping the cigar against the ashtray. "Evangeline is a very beautiful woman. Exceptional, really. But I think you're letting that five-million-dollar pussy work its way into more than just your bed."

Alistair is my friend and he means well. "I would tread carefully if I were you, Alistair," I warn.

He throws his hands in the air in mock surrender, his brows furrowed. "You know I only want good things for you," he explains, "but what happens when the contract is up?"

"About that." I get up from the chair and walk over to the patio doors looking out at the dock, Evangeline's blonde hair visible in the distance as she and Cleo sit in the Adirondack chairs. They look to be in deep conversation.

"I want you to do something for me." I turn to face him.

Alistair leans forward, all playfulness wiped from his face.

"I want you to put the money in an account for her." I walk across the room.

He looks a little too excited at the prospect. "I can do that."

"And give her access to it now."

Alistair raises his eyebrows. "Are you sure you want to do that?"

"Very much." I stop in front of the bookcase.

My father has an extensive library, ranging from history to poetry. I pluck one off the shelf and inspect it.

"Darren, as your friend, I would advise against this. You give her access to the money, she'll take it and leave."

"You don't know her!" I argue.

"You think because she looks at you like you're her savior she's gonna become a D.C. socialite?" Alistair protest.

"I'm nobody's savior, Alistair!" I run a hand through my hair. "I should have never got her fired in the first place. At least this way I can make up for it."

"I get that you feel guilty, but just giving her five million dollars?" Alistair snuffs out the cigar and stands.

"It was the agreement, and it's always been the agreement. What does it matter if she has it now or at the end of the year?" I raise my voice.

"The difference is you." He points at me. "You're different."

"Isn't that a good thing?" I place the book back on the shelf. "It's because of her that I'm different. It's because of her that I don't want to waste my life anymore."

"And I get that, but are your expectations the same as hers?" Alistair raises the question.

In my head my expectations are exactly where they should be – that this is a good thing, this will make sense in the long run because I'm creating a future for myself. But what will that future look like and with who, I don't know. Does anybody know that for certain?

"I'm not delusional, but I also don't have crystal ball, Alistair. I don't know what's going to happen. I only know what I *don't* want to happen, and I'm making steps to ensure that," I rebuke. "I cannot live in my parents shadow any longer."

"That's all very inspirational, but I don't want you to get taken advantage of." His expression softens and he adds in a quiet tone, "I don't want to see you get hurt."

I grab him by the shoulders. "I appreciate it, more than you know, but it's what I want. Can you just do that for me?"

Alistair nods. "Anything, Dare. You know that."

I nod, letting him go and turning back to the desk.

"And no offense, Alistair, but you're the last person I'd take advice from, especially coming from someone who's trying to bed his boss," I tease, trying to lighten the mood.

"None taken, but you know I've always had a fondness for older women," Alistair concedes, making his way over to the desk and looking at the pile of law books and journals. "Do you think Judge Hoskins will take you back as his clerk?"

"I think that ship sailed when you defiled his only daughter and got me fired," I emphasize.

"She was worth it," Alistair winks.

"For who?" I laugh. "Besides, I don't want to be a trial lawyer anyway." Getting fired from Hoskins clerkship was a blessing. I'd only done it to appease my father, but I had no interest in the court system.

"Then I did you a favor and that means you owe me."

I laugh and shake my head. "I don't think it works like that."

"What kind of lawyer *are* you going to be?"

I clasp my hands behind my back while I walk behind the desk. I'd been thinking about that for a while now. "I don't know yet. I just have to *pass* the Bar first, and then I'll figure it out."

"If I can pass the exam to get my series seven, then I'm sure you can pass the Bar because let's face it, I was never a good student, and you never lived up to your potential," he reminds me.

I laugh and sit on the edge of the desk with my arms crossed over my chest. I've taken the last two days off studying because of the holiday and having guests, but I find myself itching to get back at it again.

"February will be here before I know it," I sigh, picking up one of the law books and turning it over in my hand. "I will not be one of those fucks who has to take the Bar three times to pass like Rori Colton." I drop the book back on the desk making a loud slap noise.

"Who's Rori Colton?" Alistair takes a seat in one of the chairs.

"He's the candidate Rausch is backing to take my father's empty seat in Congress."

"You knew this would happen," he reminds me.

I sit behind the desk, picking up a pen and turning it over between my fingers. "Do you ever feel like life is happening around you, but you're not part of it?"

"I'm not sure what you mean."

I set the pen down and rest my forearms on the desk. "Our whole lives have been planned out for us - what preschool we went to, Cotillions, charity events, and George-town," I scoff. "We were legacies. It was shoved down our throats of what a privilege it was, and maybe it was, but legacy only means that you don't have a choice."

"I don't disagree, Dare," Alistair laughs.

"You were always better at accepting your fate than I was."

20

Because He Loved You
Evangeline

The cold air makes my lungs burn, and I can actually see my breath, tiny puffs of air suspended in front of me for only a second until they disappear. It's not something I'm used to. Twigs and pine needles litter the trail, snapping and bending under my feet. Through the thick layer of pines up ahead, I can see pieces of the lake reflecting the clouds.

Today is the first day since we arrived at the lake house that it's been cloudy, and I'm enjoying it.

Yesterday, I said goodbye to Cleo and hugged her in the driveway before she got in the car that took her to the airport, all while Alistair complained about the long drive back to Georgetown.

You won't be back, she'd said.

I run harder, pushing my legs faster. The clouds darken, covering up the sun, and in the thick woods, it makes the forest gloomy.

That boy is in love with you.

I shake my head at the word *boy*. Maybe he was a boy

when I met him – a boy who had lost his parents, drunk-quoting Emerson, and looking like a sad, tragic, beautiful boy that was nothing but trouble.

The problem was… I liked trouble.

Love.

I didn't believe in it.

With the house now coming into view, I push myself harder, wanting to finish the three-mile loop faster than I had the day before, because the more my lungs burn and the more my calves ache, the less I feel on the inside. As soon as I get to the clearing, I come to a stop and drop to my knees in the grass.

My heart pounds against my chest as if it were trying to burst through. The sky is full of tiny falling snowflakes that hit my cheeks and settle on my eyelashes until I blink them away. It's one of the most beautiful things I've ever seen.

I stand, pressing my palms against my thighs to catch my breath before standing upright. The snow melts the minute it hits the ground, but it makes the clearing look like a shaken snow globe. I can't explain the pure delight that I feel in this moment, and when I look toward the house, I find Darren standing on the deck watching me.

The damn butterflies in my stomach refuse to listen to my head.

As Darren approaches, he shoves his hands into his pockets to save them from the chilly air, and the snow settles in his messy dark hair. He looks up at the sky and the falling snow. "Announced by all the trumpets in the sky / arrives the snow…" he leaves the rest of the Emerson poem unsaid, and it never ceases to amaze me how he can pull a quote or a full poem from his memory for just the right occasion.

He settles his eyes back on me. Noticing my scrutiny he asks with a bashful smile, "What?"

"I don't know," I shake my head. "You seemed worried

148

about passing your exam, but with a memory like that, I don't see how you wouldn't."

"Alistair said something similar yesterday."

"Oh?" I laugh. "I'm not sure how I feel about having the same thoughts as Alistair," I tease.

"I'm afraid being able to quote Emerson on a whim isn't very useful in passing the Bar."

"Then why aren't you in there studying?" I scold him while rubbing my hands together for warmth.

He shrugs. "Do you not know how very distracting you are?"

"I think you find everything distracting when it's something you don't want to be doing." I raise an eyebrow.

"You look like you've never seen snow before."

"I lived in the desert my whole life." Even though my breathing is back to normal, I find that I still sound breathless. Perhaps it's the way Darren is looking at me.

"Never?"

"Once, when I was a kid," I mention, the memory taking me back. "But it was nothing like this." I hold my hands out, and snowflakes hit my palm and disappear.

"What was it like?" he surprises me by asking.

"Slush and snow piled everywhere. Plus, I was too cold to really enjoy it because I didn't have a proper winter jacket," I laugh. "Kinda turned me off to snow for a while," I admit while looking up at the sky and sticking out my tongue to try and capture one.

"If you need pointers, stay away from the yellow snow."

I shake my head and laugh at him.

"I've lived on the East coast my whole life," Darren mentions. "Snow is like taxes – inevitable and abundant."

"That's very cynical."

"I never liked the snow," he shrugs, "but you make it feel kinda magical."

"Maybe that's because it is." I step closer, running my

hands around his waist and looking up at him. "You're going to catch a cold out here without a jacket." Looping my arm through his I lead him back to the house.

We walk up the steps and enter the door to the library. I shake the snow from my hair.

"How long do you think it will last?" I stare out the door and watch as the snowfall picks up speed.

"First snow of the year is always unpredictable," I hear him say behind me, his voice sounding weary.

The library is warm, heat pouring from the vents in the floor. Unzipping my jacket, I pull it off and lay it over the back of one of the chairs before making my way across the room to the desk where Darren sits. There are a few boxes laying around that weren't here before.

"I can see it wasn't just me that was distracting you." I run my finger along the edge of the cardboard before leaning against the desk.

"Just wanted to bring a few things back to Georgetown with us," he explains.

"When is that?" I inquire, not sure that I'm ready to leave just yet.

Darren looks out the door, the snow starting to stick.

"Soon, before winter hits. I don't want to be on the roads in a storm."

I follow his gaze out the door. "Seems like winter is already here," I sigh, turning back to Darren.

He reaches into one of the boxes and grabs a stack of cards, holding them out for me.

"What's this?" I hold the cards in my hand, noticing the top one is a crayon drawing of a family.

I look over at Darren not wanting to flip through them, because even though he handed them to me, it still feels like an invasion of privacy.

"I found them in the drawer of my father's desk." He points to them, deep lines furrowed on his forehead. "I never knew him to be sentimental, and I'm not sure what to make of it that he kept all the cards I'd made him as a kid."

I turn the cards over in my hand and flip through them, but I can see clear as day what Darren can't. I hand them back to him. "Because he loved you."

"How do you know that?"

"I used to get in trouble at school to try and get my mother's attention."

Darren raises an eyebrow.

"She'd show up at school, more annoyed that she was missing her favorite show than angry at whatever I did." I shake my head, and then pierce Darren with a stare. "Even if those cards don't convince you, then trust that every time he wanted to know what you were going to do with your life, it was because he *cared* to know."

Darren takes a deep breath. "I don't like your mother very much," he says plainly, a little darkness in his eyes that causes me to shiver.

"I don't tell you these things for you to hate her."

He pierces me with angry green eyes. "In no universe where someone treated you the way she did would I *not* wish harmful things upon them."

Only Darren can threaten someone and make it sound like a nineteenth century poem.

"She was right about one thing – I did marry a rich client." I shrug and laugh at the irony, even though deep down it still stings. "Which is what she said when I told her what I did for a living." Admitting it isn't as hard as I imagined, but I can see the flames of anger in his eyes.

"Do you still talk to her?" he probes.

"Not if I can help it," I admit truthfully. "She didn't choose me, and I made peace with it a long time ago."

He slides me off the desk and onto his lap where I wrap my arms around his shoulders. "I'm sorry, I must be all sweaty and gross." Even though it was cold out, I'm still sweaty underneath my clothes.

Darren just holds me closer and smiles up at me. "As if that would ever stop me from wanting to be near you."

I run my fingers through his hair, pushing stray pieces off his forehead and look at him thoughtfully. I realize how hard it's been for him to be here, to sit in this library and go through his parents' belongings.

The police report that Rausch gave him is sitting on the edge of his desk. Tracking my gaze, he reaches over me and grabs it.

"What are you going to do with it?" I ask.

"Do I really want to be involved in all of this?"

"It's from thirty years ago. A lot can change in that amount of time."

"And yet, my father still didn't have a relationship with him or any of his family."

The fact that it was sitting on the desk and especially after going through his father's things, I can only come to one conclusion.

"You want to go there," I say, pointing to the address.

He looks up at me, and I can feel his hand grip my waist tighter. "Lynchburg is less than two hours from here."

"You don't have to do this, Darren."

"I was supposed to go with them," he admits quietly.

"And you feel guilty."

"I feel guilty for a lot of things," he admits. "Guilt I never knew until I entered this house, saw that open book and pair of glasses, as if he were coming right back to pick up where he left off. They asked me to come with them, and I said no because I went to Vegas instead." He glances at me with a knowing expression. "If I had gone, I'd have been in the helicopter with them, but maybe, just maybe, I could have…"

"You couldn't have changed anything."

"I know there was nothing I could have done. I'm not a fixer, I am someone *to be* fixed," he fumes.

I take hold of his face, forcing him to look at me. I can see all the guilt inside of him.

"Then let me fix you," I whisper, pressing my lips to his. He closes his eyes, grabbing hold of me tighter, and kisses me back.

"And you think you're not a distraction," he murmurs.

"I can leave if you want," I say while pulling away.

He pulls me back to him. "Don't you dare."

21

Gregory Allen Walker
Darren

*L*ynchburg sits at the foothills of the rugged ridges and weathered peaks of the Blue Ridge Mountains, roughly in the center of the state of Virginia. My father rarely talked about growing up here and as a kid, I just thought my father had always lived in Georgetown, or never thought about it at all. Lynchburg wasn't on the way to Clarksville, and there was never a reason to come here – until now.

I checked the address twice after looking over the small craftsman style house which looks abandoned. It wasn't simply that the owner had not kept up with repairs, but that it was simply not inhabitable. Plywood covered the windows, and several sections of roof shingles were torn up as if caught in a tornado.

No one has lived here for a while.

"When my father began his campaign, our private lives became public." I try to imagine my father living here. It's such a stark difference from the opulent Georgetown house.

His personality was too large to fit in such a small home as this.

Evangeline sits silently next to me in the passenger seat with her legs crossed and one arm draped over the armrest as she waits for me to continue.

"Some reporter interviewed one of my college professors who seemed to give a glowing account of my intellect," I laugh wearily. "One had gone so far as getting a copy of my report card from junior high."

"That sounds very invasive," Evangeline remarks with obvious annoyance.

I shrug. "There wasn't anything particularly interesting on my report card other than one teacher said that I could become preoccupied by chatting with the opposite sex and not pay attention to the lesson."

At that, Evangeline laughs, trying to politely cover her mouth given the fact that we're sitting outside what used to be my father's childhood home.

"It's true. I was distracted by Rebecca Fade," I say fondly. "She had this beautiful long red hair."

"You mean you weren't into blondes back then," she teases.

"Ah, my taste in blondes came a bit later." I cast my eyes towards her. She's wearing her hair down the way I like, her bangs pushed to the side so I can see her pretty blue eyes gazing back at me.

"I was going to ask why the media seemed so interested in *you* when it was your father who was running for office, but…"

"Then you realized who you were talking about?" I brush a fake crumb off my shoulder.

Evangeline smacks my arm playfully.

"But they ran plenty on my father too," I continue, and watch as her playfulness ebbs away.

"Even after all that digging, somehow, there was barely a mention of Lynchburg."

The smiles and laughter seemed to be swallowed up by the silence in the car.

"I wonder why that is?"

I turn back towards the house, trying to imagine what it would have looked like when my father lived here – if the shutters were painted white, or if there were flowers planted in the front yard.

I turn back toward Evangeline, resting my hand against my mouth.

"What do you think Rausch wanted you to find here?"

Shrugging, I remark, "He likes to fuck with me." I wave my hand at the abandoned house as proof. "What he said was that despite what I thought, he didn't know everything about my father."

"You don't believe that?"

"I don't know what I'm doing here or what I thought I'd find. Does it even really matter anymore?" I ask, facing her.

"He's the only family you have. If that isn't a good reason, I don't know what is."

A knock on the window startles me, and I turn to see an older woman staring back at me with a very angry expression. I roll down the window cautiously.

"If you're one of them investors looking to knock down my house and build one of those McMansions, I'm here to tell you that we don't want that in this neighborhood." She jabs her finger at me.

I shake my head. "I'm not an investor." She steps back as I open the car door and get out.

"Do you think I'm stupid?" She places both her hands on her hips and looks me up and down.

Granted, my expensive looking attire and choice of car doesn't exactly scream *humble American innocently sitting in front of an abandoned house*, so I get why she doesn't trust me, aside from me being a stranger.

"Do you know the family that used to live here?"

"Who's asking?"

I hold out my hand but she just stares at me with a weary expression. "I'm Darren Walker."

There's a flicker of recognition in her eyes but she still questions me. "That supposed to mean something?"

"I think my grandfather used to live here. Gregory Allen Walker?" I probe cautiously, the word grandfather feeling a bit forced and foreign on my tongue, which she notices.

"You think?" She rears her head back, examining me. "If he was your grandfather, then shouldn't you know if he lived here or not?"

I can't help but chuckle, and I feel sorry for any actual investor who comes to make her an offer. "I didn't know him. He had a falling out with my father a long time ago."

She looks me over again, studying my face as if she's looking for something. I suppose when her expression softens a bit, she recognizes the traits strong enough to be passed down to both my father and me.

"Yeah, I knew the Walkers. What do you want with him?"

"He came to my father's funeral." The minute I say it her posture changes, lowering her arms to her side, the angry lines disappearing from her face.

"You're Senator Kerry Walker's son?" she asks.

"You know him then."

"Everyone knows him."

I give her a hopeful smile.

"Didn't like his politics much, but I was sorry to hear that he passed," she apologizes, her southern accent becoming more prominent as if letting down her guard.

"I didn't get a chance to talk to my grandfather, and this was the last known address I have." I rub the back of my neck, wondering once again if I made the right decision coming here. My heart says no, that this house just stirs up more memories, but he's the only family I have left, and there's a part of me that wants to know him, even if it was bad – especially if it was bad, because then maybe I can finally put to rest these questions that keep me up at night.

"You really aren't here to tear down the house, are you?" she speculates, the skepticism now fully chipped away.

"No." I shake my head. "I just thought… I thought I would find some answers, I guess, but it doesn't look like this house has been lived in for a long time."

"Ethel Jackson. That's my name."

I lean down and motion into the car. "This is my wife, Evangeline." The word *wife* rolls off my tongue much easier than the word *grandfather*.

Ethel doesn't need to lean in, she just looks past me to where Evangeline sits in the car giving a little wave. "Nice to meet you," Ethel says, and then looks back at me.

"Winter storm last year." She points to the house. "Snow became too heavy and collapsed part of the roof in the back, but truth be told, this house hasn't been taken care of for a long time." She confirms what I had already suspected.

"Did you know my grandfather?" I probe tentatively, but what I really want to know is if she knew my father, but that seems almost impossible since my father left home nearly thirty years ago and presumably never looked back. Ethel might have lived in this neighborhood her whole life, but that doesn't mean she remembers him.

"He ain't lived here for about a good year now."

"Big shots been buying up homes in the neighborhood, building these monstrosities and driving up property taxes that no one around here can afford."

"Did they buy this house?" I look at it skeptically.

"They don't care what the house looks like, son. They care about the land it's on.

What am I supposed to do when I can't afford my property tax bill anymore?" she agonizes, and I can see the worry lines in her face. "This house is all I got."

"There's nothing you can do about investors buying properties as long as they buy them legitimately."

Evangeline gets out of the car and stands next to me. She looks at Ethel with concern.

"There must be something you can do," Evangeline pleads.

I sigh, rubbing the back of my neck. "Have you looked into a relief program?"

"I don't know what that is." Ethel gives me a skeptical look.

"Some states have what's called a senior freeze program. There are obviously age requirements, but if you qualify it freezes the valuation of your home," I explain.

"You think I could do that?" Her face lights up, smoothing out the worry lines on her forehead.

I feel Evangeline loop her fingers through mine.

"You'd have to see if the county has a program first."

"Sounds like a lot of red tape," she grouses, and then shakes her head in frustration. "I... I wouldn't know the first thing about how to do any of that."

"You don't have any grandkids that are computer savvy?" I inquire.

She narrows her eyes at me. "Most of them moved away. I got one all the way in California."

"You could help her." Evangeline squeezes my hand. This isn't why I came here, but with both Evangeline and Ethel giving me a wide-eyed, pleading look, I don't see how I can leave here without at least looking it up for her.

"If you help me with this relief program, I'll tell you everything I know," she offers in her best conspiratorial tone.

"I can't guarantee anything," I make sure to explain.

"Ain't nothing come with a guarantee unless it's death or taxes." Ethel rolls her eyes, and I can't help but laugh.

"Do you have a computer?"

"I might live in the country, but I'm no bumpkin. Sure, I got a computer." She waves me to follow her inside, and reluctantly I follow.

"This is very sweet of you to do," Evangeline says softy while she takes my arm, and I help her up the stairs to Ethel's house.

"Do I have a choice?"

22

You Can't Please Everyone
Evangeline

*D*arren's been quiet ever since we left Ethel's house. He's kept his eyes on the road ahead, eating up the miles as we head back towards Georgetown. The boxes containing some of his parents' things rattle in the backseat as we travel down the bumpy highway. This has been an emotional day for Darren, leaving the lake house and seeing the home his father grew up in.

"Darren?"

"I don't want to talk about it," he snaps.

"You have every right to be upset, but…"

"Evan, don't."

"Don't what?" I ask, offended. "You don't even know what I was going to say."

"Whatever it was, it doesn't matter because it's not going to make me feel better," he grits out.

I narrow my eyes at him.

"I get you're upset." I place my hand on his that rests on the shifter.

"Upset doesn't begin to cover it." He shakes his head.

"You haven't said a word since we left the house."

"I shouldn't have gone there."

"You didn't know what was going to happen, but now you do," I offer.

"My parents are gone. What does it matter now?" He looks over at me, and I hate the tortured look in his eyes.

"It matters, Darren, if it helps you move on."

"Ethel's probably going to lose her home because of Rori *fucking* Colton."

"He's not the only one who voted against that Bill."

Ethel was crushed. Even though she knew there was no guarantee, I think she was more hopeful than she let on, and when Darren found that the bill to establish the relief program had been voted down, I could tell it crushed him too, especially when he saw Lynchburg's Representative, Rori Colton, had voted against it.

"Yeah, but now he's the one taking over my father's seat in Congress," he grunts.

"Is that what really has you so upset? The thought of someone else taking your father's seat?"

"I knew his seat couldn't stay empty, but Jesus, Rori? He's..." Darren struggles to come up with something so I help him out.

"Not good enough?"

"Not when he's gonna vote to kick old ladies out of their homes," Darren laments.

"Rori's hardly the antichrist because he didn't vote the way you wanted. I'm sure he's never met Ethel or anyone in that neighborhood for that matter," I insist, trying to make him feel better, but Darren grips the steering wheel tighter, his knuckles turning white.

"That's the problem. He's supposed to serve the people of his district."

"Surely your father told you that you can't please everyone, especially in politics. There's always going to be someone who benefits and someone who doesn't, no matter how you vote," I try to explain.

"It's not just Rori or my father's empty seat – it's Ethel."

"You really do care about her, don't you?"

"Ah, you've found out my secret," he teases. "I'm a big softy when it comes to elderly southern women who threaten to hit me with a cane," he grins, but I can still see the conflict hiding in his eyes.

"Darren," I fret softly, "I think it's wonderful what you tried to do for Ethel, but some things aren't in your control."

"Maybe… I don't know. Sometimes I wish they were," he admits.

With his jaw set tight he looks sharper, older, more beautiful… like a man on fire whose embers are burning deep below the surface, and it causes the knots in my stomach to twist. It reminds me of something Rausch said, *and to think he's only scratching the surface of his potential*. That felt like such a long time ago, and here I am, looking at Darren, not seeing it but *feeling* it, like a vibration in the small space of the car. He's not scratching the surface anymore; he's breaking through, and it's incredibly sexy.

He grips the steering wheel tight, the tension causing the sinewy tendons in his arm to contract. While he focuses on the road, I reach across the console and lay my hand on his thigh, feeling the tight muscles twitch through his jeans. He looks over and smiles at me and then swallows hard when he feels my hand caress his cock. I feel it jump in response, and Darren clears his throat.

When I unbutton his pants, he grips the steering wheel tighter – his knuckles turning white.

"Evan," he warns, glancing over at me, but I don't listen and reach inside, dipping my hand under his boxers to feel him already getting hard.

I wrap my hand around his length and Darren shifts in his seat. When I unclip my seatbelt, Darren tenses.

"You shouldn't – uh, you shouldn't do that," he stammers while I lean over and take him in my mouth. "Oh, Jesus, Evan."

I like this Darren, a little nervous, a little scandalized, and I take advantage of that, taking him deep. The sound of his breath hitching and the feel of his hand in my hair sends a pulse right down my center – needy and bright, like a flame licking up my insides.

I move up and down his shaft, sucking and licking, tasting the saltiness of his precum, knowing that he's close. His stomach trembles while his grip in my hair tightens – pushing me further to take him deeper. His hips shift, the involuntary need to pump, to seek out more, and I'm happy to give it to him.

"Fuck," he rasps breathlessly.

Darren curses right before the car spins, and I'm thrown back in my seat, clutching for my seatbelt.

"Evan!" I hear Darren's voice, and everything seems to snap back into place. We're in a ditch on the side of the road, and once the shock wears off, I can't help but laugh.

"I'm sorry," I manage to sputter out. "I didn't mean to…"

I don't get to finish my sentence because Darren reaches for me, pulling me over the console and onto his lap. "You don't get to start something and not finish it," he scolds before kissing me.

The thrum of his pulse vibrates against my lips in a scorching kiss. His hand snakes up my back, pushing me harder against him. He moans into my mouth, and I run my hands along his shoulders and into his hair, pulling on the strands.

Desperate and without a word, I reach between us to find that he's still hard, and I hum at the feel of him in my hand, thick and swelling. While I knead his cock, he pulls open the buttons of my shirt, dipping his hand into my bra and pulling one of my breasts out. He takes my nipple into his mouth, and I let go of his cock so I can lean back further against the steering wheel as he nips his way from one breast to the other, all while grinding into his lap.

I lower my head back to him, my eyelids heavy. "Darren," I whine, and as if hearing the desperation in my voice, he moves his seat back as far as it will go and then he turns me over on his lap, so my back is to him. I can feel his cock press against me, and he unbuttons my jeans and dips his hand into my panties.

"Oh, God," he rasps, pressing hungry kisses to my neck while palming one of my breasts. I lean my head back to rest against his shoulder while I moan and greedily move my hips to meet his fingers while they pump in and out of me.

"Anyone could walk up to the car," he whispers, his voice heavy with lust, "looking to see if we're okay. Is that what you want?" His voice is like a low rumble against my ear, and hot breath caresses my neck making me even more needy.

I'm unable to speak because the feverish movements of his fingers inside me render me speechless. His broken breaths against my neck and the way his hand trembles while he cups my breast tells me he needs me to come just as much as I do.

I tilt my head to try and meet his mouth, wanting to kiss him, to taste him, to have any part of him. Even though the windows are up, I can still hear the soft hum of the highway next to us. The wind from a semi-truck passing by rocks the car, and it mimics my own rocking against his fingers.

Pent up lust is knotting inside my cunt, and the need to come is overwhelming. His fingers dip into me, spreading my wetness along my slit, and when he teases my clit, I'm so sensitive that I can't help but shiver and shake.

"Darren," I whine, begging him for more.

"Jesus, Evan." He hastily pushes my jeans down, along with my panties, and I step out of them as best I can in the restrictive space between him and the steering wheel. When I turn around, I find him hard and dripping, and God, so ready.

He's holding his cock in position for me to slide down on him. The minute I do I moan with satisfaction at the fullness and the pressure against my walls. I can't stop, and the faster I move the more needy I become, desperate to relieve the building ache that threatens to slice me in half.

While he pumps his hips to meet me, I grind my clit against the ridges of his hard stomach. "That's right, Queenie." His breathless voice urges me on. "Take it," he coaxes and I'm so very close, so desperately close.

He grips my hips, pushing and pulling me at a frantic pace. I'm almost there, my orgasm about to crest when I open my eyes and look down at him. He's staring up at me with eyes that can't decide whether they want to be green or brown, as I fall apart around him. His lashes flutter closed, his mouth parts but no sound comes out, and then he bites down on his lip as if to hold in a moan.

I can feel the walls of my pussy contract, gripping him tighter as he thrusts into me harder, letting go of his own release. He wraps his arms around me and reaches for my mouth while our bodies slow and the endorphins ebb away. I smile against his mouth, my teeth grazing his bottom lip.

"Jesus, Evan," he groans, his voice rough and raw, drawing me in. "Why do you feel so goddamn good? Every. Fucking. Time."

I push a few strands of dark, wavy hair from his forehead, still breathing heavily when Darren looks over my shoulder – his eyes going wide.

"Shit!" he barks, nudging me to move off him and he hands my pants to me. "Hurry, put these on."

23

Ice On The Road
Darren

*A*fter I finish pushing my semi-hard dick back in my pants, I run a hand through my hair and step out of the car, leaving Evangeline inside to finish dressing.

"Everyone alright?" the officer asks, looking over the car that I hadn't even had a chance to assess what, if any, damage had happened after careening off the highway.

The car sits in the uneven section of dirt and grass on the side of the highway. I can't help but notice how close we are to the crop of trees.

"Yeah, just a little ice on the road."

The cop, who looks to be around the same age as me, looks over the vehicle with a skeptical eye. "Anyone been drinking?" he questions.

I shake my head. "No." Which is actually true. If he'd have asked me any other time, I don't think I'd be able to safely say that I would pass a breathalyzer test. In fact, I can't remember the last time I'd had a drink.

"Anyone else in the vehicle?" He looks through the back window, but the tint prevents him from seeing inside.

He heads to the passenger side and my armpits start to sweat as I follow him.

"My wife." I meet him just as she opens the door, jeans on, shirt buttoned, hair a little windblown, but fucking gorgeous as usual.

She steps out of the vehicle and I hold my hand out to her while the cop looks her over.

"Is everything okay?" She looks between me and the cop.

"We got reports that someone fitting this vehicle's description was driving erratically on the freeway," he states.

I try hard not to roll my eyes while the cop tries to look through the open door, but I shut it. Not that I have anything to hide, but I don't need this to be on the evening news – I can almost see the headline, *senator's son arrested for fucking his wife on side of road*.

"Ice on the road, like I said."

"Do you mind if I search the car?"

I've done nothing wrong, and he can't prove that I was the one driving erratically. If I protest, it'll make this take longer and I just want to get home.

"Go ahead." I wave at the car.

"Anything in here I should know about first?" he inquires, and I'm not sure what he's expecting to find, but it is the south.

"No, I mean, not unless you're going to write up a ticket for being messy," I joke, but his straight face tells me he's not in the joking mood.

Evangeline and I lean against the trunk of the car while he starts poking around.

I give Evangeline an annoyed look.

"What?"

"If you had kept your greedy hands to yourself..." I shake my head, but I can't help noticing how sexy she looks when she's freshly fucked.

"Then I wouldn't have had the best car fuck of my life." She gives me a not so innocent grin.

"You fuck in cars often?" I raise a discerning eyebrow.

"Don't you?" she questions, sarcastically.

I shake my head and laugh, crossing my arms over my chest. My wife is dirty and I love it.

"I'm trying to be a respectable man of society, but you keep corrupting me," I tease, unable to keep the grin off my face.

"I was trying to take your mind off things," she shrugs.

"You certainly accomplished that."

Evangeline hooks her thumb towards the cop. "Should I call Alistair to pick you up from jail?" she muses with a sweet but cunning smile.

"You wouldn't dare!"

"I bet he'd like that. Return the favor and all." She folds her arms over her chest.

"He would gloat about it for weeks – months maybe," I groan.

Evangeline shakes her head and laughs.

I look towards the trees again noticing they're only a few feet away. "I wouldn't have been able to live with myself if something happened to you."

"I know." She lays a hand on my arm and the heat of her palm cuts through the chilly winter air.

"I'm sorry you didn't get the answers you wanted," she apologizes.

"It's not your fault." I scratch the back of my head. "I guess I was hoping Ethel had a long memory, but even she didn't know much about the arrest."

"Maybe it's not important. Maybe it doesn't have anything to do with why your father didn't speak to him," she pauses. "Sometimes there isn't any one defining moment, but a culmination of events in which parents disappoint us."

Evangeline knows this better than anyone and maybe

she's right. I'm focusing on something that doesn't matter anymore. "I just thought if I knew, I'd have a better understanding of my father." I shrug.

The car door shuts, and I hear the crunch of the officer's shoes on the gravel as he rounds the car.

"I could arrest you for public indecency, but…"

"What?" I can't help how high pitch my voice sounds.

"If you want to have sex, I suggest finding a hotel room, not the side of the highway," he warns modestly. He looks at Evangeline and his cheeks turn an unnatural shade of pink, and not because of the crisp winter air.

"I don't know what you're talking about," I scoff, shaking my head.

"Panties on the floorboard say otherwise."

I raise my eyebrows. "You didn't put your panties back on?" I ask through gritted teeth.

She shrugs apologetically. "I didn't have time."

"Look, I have better things to do then arrest people for having a little fun in their car," the officer explains. "However, if I catch you driving like a lunatic on my highway again, I won't hesitate to give you a reckless driving ticket."

I roll my eyes and slump against the trunk of the car.

The officer gets back in his truck, and as soon as he merges onto the highway, Evangeline doubles over in fits of giggles.

"You find this amusing?" I ask, but I can't help liking the sound of her girlish giggles.

"The look on your face was priceless when he said public indecency! Oh, God, I thought you were going to faint," she giggles.

I tug her close to me, feeling her body shake against mine.

"Be careful, Evangeline, or I will fuck that sweet cunt of yours while I bend you over the trunk."

"You wouldn't dare," she tests me.

"It would be worth a hundred tickets."

24

About The Agreement
Evangeline

*B*eing back in Washington is like being thrown back into the hornet's nest. Clarksville felt like a safe bubble, but I knew it was time to get back to reality, or at least my version of it. That meant attending the first Board meeting of the new year for the Abigail Pershing Foundation.

I thought it was more of an informal meeting, maybe not folding chairs in a circle, but something adjacent. I'm not sure why I would even consider that with someone as poised and elegant as Audrina Ellwood running it.

As if proximity to the Supreme Court and the Shakespeare Library weren't daunting enough, Bethany York is making a beeline straight towards me.

"Evangeline!" She takes me by the shoulders and gives me a light peck on the cheek, careful not to transfer her perfectly pale pink lipstick onto me. Her genuine enthusiasm at my arrival puts me at ease, and when she notices my knee-length pencil skirt and heels, she smiles her approval.

"How was your holiday?" she inquires, leading me into

the conference room. "Darren said you went to the lake house."

"Yes, it was very nice. It's so beautiful there." I set my purse on the table.

"I remember when they first built the cabin and we all went down for the weekend to break it in. Merrill had a good eye for decorating, and she would host the most sublime dinner parties," Bethany beams, but there's always a bit of sadness in her tone when she tells stories about Merrill.

"Well, I'm afraid I'm not as good a hostess as Merrill, but we all did manage to have a nice Thanksgiving," I offer.

"I don't think Darren would care if he ate dinner from a taco stand every night, so long as it was with you," she surprises me by saying.

"Thank God we have Lottie, because as much as I love tacos, I don't think I could have them every night," I laugh.

"You and me both," Bethany winks.

"I hope you're not laughing at me! Dupont Circle is always such a mess, and I'm sorry I'm late." Audrina leans in to give Bethany a kiss on her cheek, then does the same with me.

"We wouldn't dream of it," Bethany teases. "Just laughing at our lack of homemaking skills."

"Don't ever go to Bethany's for dinner unless it's catered," Audrina advises as she shucks her jacket and drapes it over the back of the chair.

"I will never live that down," Bethany sighs.

"The duck was raw," Audrina lets me in on the joke.

"Well, I'm not Martha Stewart that's for sure, but I suppose now I'll have time to learn," Bethany jests.

"How long did you work for the National Archives Museum?" I probe.

Beside Bethany being an intimidating force, she's also a very interesting person that I'd like to get to know better.

"Nearly thirty years. I was fortunate enough to get an

internship while I was in college, and then I was hired on after I graduated."

"That must have been a wonderful career." I can't help but feel a small pebble of jealousy. I loved the idea of being a journalist, but there was so much out there I hadn't experienced. Lately, I've allowed myself to wonder what a different kind of life would be like. I'd been so focused on taking care of Mimi that I never wondered what I could do with my own life, especially with the money I'm about to acquire.

"It saw me through two divorces, so I suppose it was the only thing that was constant and loyal," Bethany jests, bringing me out of my own thoughts.

"Oh, I'm sorry to hear that," I offer.

"Don't be. My first marriage… I was young and stupid, and when he got a job offer in California and I didn't want to leave Washington, that was the end of that," she says sadly. "The first one always stings the worst."

"Bethany has always been a career woman," Audrina offers teasingly, but I don't sense any condescension, only a playfulness.

"How wonderful it must have been to work in the same building as so many priceless documents. I think it would be magical," I admit, knowing I sound a bit naïve at the thought of spending all day in dusty archives with the musty smell of old paper. Being able to look at the Emerson letters and the Declaration of Independence sparked a fire inside me that I had been missing for so long.

I might have had some misgivings about working on the charity, but they've been nothing but welcoming.

"Are you looking for a job?" Bethany wonders as she lays out a binder on the table in front of each seat.

"Oh, no, I just meant how wonderful it was for you."

She laughs. "I'm not offering you my old job, but having your own life outside of being a Walker will be challenging.

Darren will find his way eventually, and when he does, there will be no limits," Bethany finishes.

"Audrina!" A middle-aged woman with brown hair pulled into a tight bun approaches. They give each other a peck on the cheek. "I trust you had a lovely holiday," she chatters, shucking off her jacket and laying it over the back of the chair.

"We managed to get out of Washington for a short vacation." She looks in my direction. "Oh, have you met Evangeline? This is Darren Walker's wife."

I extend my hand while Audrina introduces her to me. "This is Rebecca Langley."

My hand falters but Rebecca grabs onto me, shaking politely. Of course, I knew Senator Langley had a wife, but I never expected to be in the same room as her. Washington is very small, and the room feels even smaller.

"Very nice to meet you," Rebecca assures, and all I can do is nod.

Audrina offers me a seat next to her while she calls the meeting to order. All the board-members are wives of prominent figures in Washington which I shouldn't be surprised about, but still am.

I listen in while the treasurer walks everyone through recent donations and plans for how the money will be spent. Most of it goes to practical things like insurance and operating expenses for the safe houses. It was always my desire to be more hands-on, and finding out the Compton House, named after Merrill's family, is not too far away, I'm excited to talk to Audrina about putting in some time there.

I certainly don't have any experience with finances or party planning, and when one of the members start discussing legalities of setting up a new charter, I'm just completely out of my depth. I can't help but look across the table at Rebecca and wonder if she knows who's she married to. Does she care? It's not something I ever thought of before, even knowing ninety-nine percent of my clients were married. But I've never had to come face to face with one of their wives.

When the meeting is over, I want to linger so I can speak to Audrina about Compton House, but I don't want to speak to Rebecca again.

"This isn't really your thing, is it?" Bethany asks, stopping me from leaving while she gathers up her belongings.

"Was it that obvious?" I laugh, but inside I'm a little embarrassed that Bethany picked up on it.

"Don't worry, I get the same look when Lisbeth goes over the numbers," she teases in an attempt to make me feel better about the Treasurer's presentation.

"I really appreciate the opportunity, but I really don't think serving on the Board is my place. I know you were hoping to have someone from the family take over, but I don't think that's me," I apologize, hoping I haven't disappointed her.

"I can understand. It is a lot to get used to in such a short amount of time."

"However, I am very interested in learning more about the Compton House. I think that's where I can have the most impact," I offer.

Bethany surprises me by putting an arm around my shoulders, tugging me into her side in an almost motherly way. "I think Merrill would have really liked that. She spent a lot of time there."

Bethany tracks my gaze to Audrina who is engaged in a conversation.

"I hate to disappoint her."

Bethany waves me off. "Don't worry about Audrina, I'll handle her."

I gather my purse.

"Let's have lunch next week, and I can give you the

details." She kisses me lightly on the cheek before releasing me.

As I pass Audrina, she says, "Thank you, dear. We'll catch up soon."

I wait by the elevators, practically bouncing on my feet. I can't wait to get home and tell Darren about it.

I'm distracted so much by my thoughts of Darren that when the elevator doors open, I rush in, not paying attention and run right into Senator Jonathan Langley.

At first, I don't even recognize him and apologize. I look up at his steely blue eyes and a sick feeling starts in my belly and spreads out to my limbs.

"Excuse me." I try to walk around him, but he stops me.

"Did you really think you could pretend to be a Washington housewife?" he asks.

"I'm not pretending to be anything."

"Darren's lucky I didn't press charges." He looks me up and down.

"Let's not forget you were the one handling me," I remind him.

"I could see right through you all those years ago. You picked the wrong target, but Darren? Well, you're more his type," Jonathan sneers, and all pretense is wiped away.

"I highly doubt you care anything about my agenda," I boldly say back to him. "I think you were jealous that Kerry was a better man than you are, and Darren," I pause, "well, he'll be ten times the man you could ever be."

He laughs. "Do you think that Darren will get anywhere in politics once the public finds out what you are?" he threatens. "If he knows what's good for him, he'll cut you loose, but we all know what head Darren thinks with."

"I guess that gives me the advantage."

"You'll be his downfall." As if he can see right through me, he continues, "And I think you know it too."

"Senator Langley," I hear Audrina's voice from behind

and I cringe, hoping she didn't hear any of that. I don't care what Jonathan thinks of me, but I'd be crushed to have Audrina think I was taking advantage of Darren.

"Audrina, so nice to see you," Jonathan plasters on his politician's smile and greets her as if he didn't just say the most hurtful things to me.

But Audrina doesn't extend her hand for him to shake and there is no smile, not even a fake one, on her lovely face.

"I'm sure you've heard the saying about people who live in glass houses shouldn't throw stones." Audrina gives him a saccharin smile, and when he starts to protest, she says, "I believe your wife is waiting for you in the conference room."

She turns to me. "I didn't get a chance to introduce the two of you properly, but Mrs. Langley is quite accomplished. Her family owns hotels all over the U.S and Europe."

Jonathan clears his throat. "Yes, uh, she's very fortunate."

"Oh, I think you're the fortunate one," Audrina continues. "Rebecca is lovely, isn't she?" She gives me a very satisfied smile. If I didn't know any better, I'd think she was getting a kick out of making Jonathan squirm.

"Oh, but I guess you've had your accomplishments too," she playfully taps his arm. "Especially coming from that small town in Arizona. Such a rags-to-riches story."

Redness starts creeping up his neck.

"Yes, well, Rebecca's waiting. Pleasure as always," he says tightly, and walks past us.

As soon as he's out of earshot I begin, "Audrina, if you're wondering if I'm a gold digger, you're wrong. I married Darren for his winning personality and his work ethic."

She lifts an eyebrow. "Well, I knew you and Darren were well suited. It's that attitude: *I don't give a shit what anyone thinks.*"

"Something like that." I shift uncomfortably on my heels.

"I know you're not a gold digger, dear. Washington is very small. People talk. If you were only interested in his money,

179

I'm sure you would have traded in that – *ring* – for something a bit more appropriate by now," she offers, and I lift my hand to run my thumb over the band.

"It's kinda grown on me." I set my arm back down. "I'm betting you're very good at reading people."

Audrina graces me with a half-smile, which is encouraging. "I think that might be something we have in common."

"Senator Langley and I, well, there's history," I explain as best I can, because I think I owe her that.

Audrina lets out a breath. I'm sure she thinks I'm referring to what happened at the charity event, but she doesn't ask.

"Reputation is worth more than trust funds in Washington," Audrina explains. "Jonathan should do well to remember that."

Whoever she thinks I am and whatever history she thinks I have with Jonathan… she's reminding me that I have more of an upper hand than I thought I did. I can't let him intimidate me.

"Understood."

"Besides, I don't take kindly to one of my friends being spoken to in that way, Senator or not," she declares pointedly.

I look at her thoughtfully, an unlikely ally, and I appreciate her even more. "Thank you."

"As long as Darren is happy," she remarks, "and you're happy," she adds, which makes my heart feel full.

I grab the next elevator, and Bailey is waiting at the curb. He opens the door for me, and to my surprise, Darren is waiting for me. He must see the look on my face because his smile falters. I slide into the backseat and kiss him. He doesn't hesitate, pulling me into his lap. The excitement I had earlier at telling Darren about Compton House was overshadowed by my run-in with Langley.

He pulls away enough to ask. "Was the Board meeting that bad?"

I debate whether I want to tell him. It might just provoke him even more into doing something rash.

"Evan?" he says my name like a warning, as if he can tell I'm holding something back.

"I ran into Langley at the elevators," I admit. "Quite literally," I add and notice how Darren's body stiffens.

His silence is unnerving. "Don't do anything stupid, please."

"That depends," he grits out.

"Depends on what?" I slide off his lap as Bailey pulls the car into traffic, but his hand remains on my thigh, holding me close to him.

"A lot of factors."

He pulls my leg into his lap and tugs the heel off my foot, letting it drop to the floor and then does the same to other one.

"You know I'm going to have to put them back on to walk into the house," I tell him.

"Not if I carry you inside." He gives me a wicked smile.

"Darren." I place a hand on his chest. He covers it with his own, running his finger over my wedding band. I hadn't let Darren get me a new one because there really wasn't a point – was there?

I try to move my hand away, but Darren stops me.

"Tell me what happened," he prods in a very calm, un-Darren-like manner.

"Nothing I couldn't handle, and Audrina interrupted before it got too far," I offer. "She really cares about you, Darren. You may have lost your parents, but you still have people looking out for you."

"I don't think I'm the only one they're looking out for." He runs his hand along my leg and under my skirt.

"Not if Audrina thinks I'm a gold-digger."

"Did she say that?"

"No, Langley did, but Audrina overheard," I sigh. "And

you never told me his wife was on the Board." I smack his arm.

"If I knew, do you think I would have offered for you to be a part of it?" Darren asks tightly.

"It just threw me off is all." I relax, resting my head against his shoulder. "But I don't think I want to be on the Board, Darren."

He shifts enough so he can look down at me. "Don't let Langley intimidate you, I'm sure not."

I'm afraid to ask what he means by that.

"No, it's just that I realized I'm not really suited for that, but there was a mention of the Compton House. I think that's something I'd really like to do." I settle against him again, feeling the rattle of the car as we travel through D.C.

"I'm familiar with it." His chest rumbles against my ear.

"So, then you're okay with it?"

"Of course." His hand circles my thigh, dangerously close to my panty line.

"Can I ask something of you in return?" he requests, and I sit up, feeling the seriousness of it.

"I want you to meet with Alistair." Before I can ask why, he stops me. "About the agreement."

25

The Bat Cave
Evangeline

hitlock Capital, in large chrome letters, is displayed prominently behind the receptionist's desk. Floor to ceiling windows provide a beautiful view of the Potomac, and the lobby is decorated in whites and cool blues matching the landscape. Behind the big glass doors is the heart of the office, rows of desks with every computer screen displaying stock graphs and numbers.

"Evangeline Bowen, I mean Walker, to see Alistair Van Der Walt," I announce to the receptionist sitting behind the desk. She matches the office with a tight, high ponytail of dark brown hair, and a crisp white collared button up shirt.

She looks up from her computer. "Alistair?" she questions as if I have the wrong person.

"Yes, I have an appointment."

She barks into the phone, "Van de Walt, your appointment is here."

Motioning to the plush white couches, she offers, "You can take a seat while you wait."

"Thank you," I smile, and notice the modern art hanging

on the walls. I step a little closer, admiring the brush strokes and colors. It's a contrast of color against the stark white wall, but perhaps that's on purpose so it stands out.

The receptionist notices me eying the paintings. "That one's a Brodinsky. Mr. Whitlock is a collector."

"It's beautiful." Darren has one hanging in the hallway of our home – his home, but I don't say that out loud.

I make my way to the couch, but before I can take a seat, Alistair comes bounding through the glass double doors.

He's wearing a tailored suit and tie that makes him look very dashing.

"Evangeline, nice to see you," he greets me in a profes-sional manner that I'm not used to. "Do you want coffee, or maybe some water?" he offers sweetly. "Jordan will get you anything you need." He motions to the receptionist.

"I'm fine."

Jordan makes a face at him.

"Let's go back to my office." He holds the door open for me, and we walk into the heart of the office.

It's noisy and smells like coffee. I watch as people rush by, phones to their ears, ties loosened, and half eaten food in containers left abandoned on desks.

"Wow, Alistair, you really grew up," I comment as we pass a wide staircase that leads to the second floor where executives must work, just judging by the square footage of the offices that I can see.

"I'm no longer playing in the kindergarten sandbox," he winks, holding the door to his office while I pass through. He loosens his tie and takes a seat behind his desk.

"Adulthood is treating you well." I admire his office, decorated in dark woods and light carpeting. On the opposite wall is a framed certificate. "It's a beautiful office."

"You can put lipstick on a pig, but it's still a pig," Alistair jokes. "It's still a job," he shrugs.

"Your receptionist is nice. She seems to like you," I say sarcastically, judging by her attitude towards him.

"She's so far up Whitlock's ass, she smells like money," Alistair jokes, motioning behind me. A man wearing jeans and a graphic t-shirt of a band I don't recognize, is on the second floor, looking down at the hustle of the office.

"He looks young to be running a firm like this," I note. "Darren said he was a friend of your father's."

"That's his son. Everyone calls him Lock. He took over the firm a few years ago," Alistair explains.

"Does he always dress like that at work?" I'm trying not to judge, but with a company this size and serving most of Washington's elite, I would have thought he'd be in a suit and tie like Alistair.

"He's a bit unconventional. Reminds me of Darren, rebelling against the patriarch," Alistair offers.

"By the way, where is Darren?" Alistair raises a questioning eyebrow.

"Studying."

Alistair make a noise of agreement.

"This looks like the bat cave." I gesture to the five monitors lined up on his desk and the TV mounted on the wall with the sound turned off.

"I assure you, there's no saving of Gotham happening here," he explains in a foreboding manner.

Alistair sits back in his chair, casually crossing one ankle over the other and inspects his tie as if he didn't realize he had one on. His blond hair is no longer the carefree locks of a boy who plays lacrosse, but rather the carefully wrangled strands of a man who is lording over Gotham.

"I opened an account for you. The money is accessible for however you want to use it, but if I can suggest…"

"Those weren't the terms," I interrupt.

"I know Darren wasn't exactly excited about me handling

the money, but I assured him I would take very good care of you."

"And that included having access to the money before the contract was up?" I question.

"You didn't know?" He tilts his head curiously.

I shake my head. "Darren neglected to provide that detail."

"Well, he explicitly told me that you were to have access to whatever you needed," he explains.

I don't know whether to be angry at him or relieved. I'd already been going through my savings as it was.

"I doubt this is the kind of thing your firm deals with."

"You'd be surprised." He smooths the tie against his chest and leans forward.

Getting back down to business, he pulls up something on his computer and tilts the screen in my direction so I can see. "I can invest the money however you like, but I have some options that could make you a modest profit, depending on how risky or conservative you want to be."

"I don't need it to make money," I insist exasperatedly. "I mean, five million is more than anyone would need."

Alistair flips a pen around between his fingers while giving me a challenging stare.

"That's not what we do here."

"So, what exactly do you do?" I inquire.

"Make the rich richer, of course." He says it as if it's a given, but I suppose a firm like this isn't for someone who has only a hundred dollars to invest – probably not even a thousand. I raise my eyebrows. "I'm not looking to be richer."

"You don't have a choice because it's my fiduciary duty to invest your money wisely," he informs me.

Alistair and *duty* were two words I never thought would be uttered in the same sentence, but then again, I never thought I'd be sitting on the opposite side of a desk having options on how to invest five million dollars. The thought makes me swallow hard. I know I asked for it – demanded it really – but I didn't think much about what it would look like to have it.

"And the more money I make, the more money you make." I stare back at him.

"That's a given." He sets the pen down.

A ruckus in the office distracts me, and I turn around to see a group of men enter the center of the bullpen where a small basketball hoop is erected under the railing of the second floor.

They lift one of the guys, who slams a basketball through the hoop as they cheer. From the second floor, Lock watches with amusement.

I turn back to Alistair. "What's that all about?"

He rubs the back of his neck as if he doesn't want to tell me, but he does anyway. "When someone brings in a particularly wealthy client, you get a slam dunk." His cheeks turn rosy with embarrassment.

I turn back to watch as they congregate under the hoop.

"Will you get a slam dunk for bringing me in?" I speculate.

His cheeks turn an even brighter shade of pink. "To be frank, five million barely gets you a pat on the back here." He raises an eyebrow.

This is a world that I don't understand and simply don't belong in, because five million dollars is life altering to the point that it makes me queasy. To think it means nothing to them – Alistair included – just makes me feel even more over my head. I stand to leave, but Alistair quickly rises from his chair, rounding the desk to stop me.

"I didn't mean to upset you."

I shake my head, grabbing my purse.

"Please, don't leave."

"I don't know why I came here to begin with."

"I'm just being honest with you. I don't want you to have

any pretense about what we're doing here, and who you're doing business with," he explains, and I can see the sincerity in his face.

"Look, it's more than just my ethical obligation to do the right thing by you."

"It's because I'm Darren's wife," I say for him.

"No," he states resolutely. "It's because I care about you." He crosses his arms over his chest. "I might have had a hand in everything that went down in Vegas, but do not think that I was ever okay with it, and the more I got to know you, the more it weighed on my conscience."

"You might think I accepted the offer too eagerly, Alistair, but you're wrong."

"I have never thought that about you."

I raise an eyebrow.

"Truthfully, I advised Darren not to give you access to the money before the contract was up."

I purse my lips. "I suppose that's fair."

"Look, however you came into this money is irrelevant. Here, you're a number, and that's not a bad thing if you're looking for anonymity."

I sit back in the chair, placing my purse in my lap.

"If you let me manage your money, I will make sure that, whatever the reason you accepted it, it will be more than enough to sustain you for a long time to come."

"I just want to make sure my grandmother has the best care."

Alistair sits back, intrigued. "Okay, tell me about your grandmother."

26

Very Different View
Darren

*I*t's getting closer to the exam date, and I've been spending hours each day trying to cram in as much information as I can. I massage my forehead, hoping it'll relieve the headache that's starting to form. The bar review course I purchased has been immensely helpful, but staring at the computer for hours at a time wears on my eyes.

"You look good behind your father's desk," Rausch says from the doorway as he makes his way inside.

He shoves his hands in the pockets of his dress pants and looks around at the small changes I've made.

I packed away some of his personal effects, and the degrees and recognitions that hung on the walls. However, I couldn't bring myself to remove the framed Emerson poem. It still hangs on the wall behind me, and Rausch's eyes settle upon it as he stands in front of the desk.

"Very different view from this side," I lean forward.

"Very different indeed." He takes a seat and crosses his legs.

"I think this is the first time we've been in the same room together without yelling at each other."

"Why do you suppose that is?" he queries, a knowing smile on his face.

Perhaps my aversion to sparring is because I need something from him.

Instead of answering his question, I get right to the point. "I went to the house in Lynchburg."

His lips are pressed tight as he waits for me to continue.

"I'm sure you knew he didn't live there anymore." I don't need him to confirm it.

"I suspect he is a transient." Once again, he neither admits nor denies that he knows anything. I simply don't care anymore.

"I met his neighbor, Ethel." He makes no indication that he knows her, so I continue.

"Did you know that Rori Colton voted down a bill to freeze property taxes for seniors?" I ask, the echo of anger still vibrating through me.

"The Governor has already made his decision, there is nothing you can…"

"I don't give a shit if he takes my father's seat. I do, however, give a shit about Ethel and her neighbors who can't pay their property taxes," I raise my voice slightly.

"I'm not following you here." He clasps his hands in his lap, as if settling in for a long tale.

"Investors are driving up property taxes, and there was a relief bill that none of their representatives voted for."

"Careful, Darren, or people might think you actually care about someone besides yourself."

I laugh. "To you, politics is about having control," I accuse because the *real* selfish one is Rausch. "Not following the interests of your constituents."

"Is that what you think your father did?" he accuses me. "Follow his own interests?"

His question catches me off guard.

"I think he went into politics for pure reasons, but," I falter, because even I don't want to admit that I looked up to my father my whole life, but that politics had corrupted him and party lines forced him into decisions he didn't want to make. I knew this, not because he confided in me, but the ever-present conflict in his eyes, the tiny crow's feet, and the clench of his jaw told me that story every time I looked at him, "that won't be me." Even as I say it, I know how naïve that makes me sound.

A careful smile spreads on his face.

I rise from the chair and round the desk, but instead of leaning on its edge, I walk over to the bookshelf. "Did you know that I was trying to get laid after a bump of coke and way too many drinks when someone turned on the TV and I saw the mangled helicopter?"

Rausch makes an indignant noise.

"I was so inconsequential that no one called me."

"Darren, I tried calling you but you wouldn't pick up," Rausch offers, turning in his chair to face me with an apologetic look on his face.

"You knew the minute the helicopter went down." It's not a challenge, nor am I looking for confirmation. "You knew before the press, even before the fucking ambulance driver."

"Darren…" he sighs like a warning not to tempt him into telling the truth, because sometimes the truth can be unbearable.

But I have to know.

"What was more important than warning me?" I question, turning away from him and looking at the bookshelf again in order to give myself some space.

"Am I not allowed to grieve?" He stands abruptly. I see the pain in his eyes that he's always so careful to hide. I know that look, because I see it in the mirror every morning.

For a moment, I'm taken aback by his sudden rush of rare

emotion; as if his heavy plates of armor have been stripped off unwillingly – aggressively. The moment is so heavy the air feels charged in this office, in the place where my father's presence still lingers like the scent of aftershave long after its use.

"I was his son!" I yell, giving into my emotions.

"Do you think that your grief trumps everyone else's?" Rausch demands.

"Yes!" I raise my arms in the air. "That's how it works, Rausch. It is my blood, my legacy, and I had a right to know before anyone else."

Rausch casts his eyes to the ground and pinches the bridge of his nose.

He slumps back into his chair and adjusts his tie. "I was in shock," he explains, in a cool, and careful manner. "I tried to hold off the press…"

But he doesn't finish the sentence because it doesn't change what happened. It will never take back the pain in that moment when I saw the news, but it doesn't overshadow the fact that my parents are no longer here.

"I regretted being in Vegas when I should have been at the lake house with them, on the helicopter with them." Rausch's eyes snap to mine. "And when my friends wouldn't leave the suite, I did."

I take my seat behind the desk once more, feeling the weight of it – always feeling the weight of it. Rausch sits on the other side, rapt with attention, and surprisingly no condescension in his stare.

"I went into the bar intent on drinking myself into a state where I wasn't burdened with the knowledge that I was *alone*. When I got thrown out and I was sitting in that alley, I realized that the only two people in this world that would miss me if I ceased to exist, didn't exist anymore themselves."

His expression turns to one of sadness, and dare I say, maybe a bit of understanding.

"And the only person who cared enough to see if I was okay was a fucking hooker, as you so gently called her. She could have left me that night, I'd already paid her, but she didn't, because I'd kicked Alistair out, and if she left, there would be no one there to know if I had aspirated in my fucking sleep! And how did I repay her?" I ask, feeling a heaviness in my chest that gnaws at me still. "I got her fired from her agency so she'd need the money I offered her to marry me."

There's a deep crease in his brow.

"Darren, I didn't—" His voice is low and laced with remorse.

"You didn't need to know in order to treat her with respect. Even after all of that, do you know where she is right now?"

Rausch sits perfectly still, his fingers laced together in his lap.

"She's delivering necessities and clothing to Compton House." I jab my finger against the wood desk forcefully enough to cause a jolt of pain to run through my knuckle. "My *mother's* charity." I don't need to mention all of the other things she's done since she got here, because I don't need to explain what a good person she is to him. Whether he believes me or not is irrelevant, but he will treat her with some modicum of respect.

"I might have paid her to marry me, but I didn't pay her to be a good person."

"I'm sorry, Darren," he apologizes in an unsettlingly quiet voice.

"I didn't tell you that to garner an apology," I explain, and he tilts his head in confusion. "I told you, because…" I falter, unsure myself why I needed to tell him, "because I needed to say it out loud."

Saying it out loud makes it real. My truth of that night.

A knowing smile settles on Rausch's face, but it's not

sinister or malicious. It's the smile of a man who has worked out a puzzle, putting the last piece into place. I wonder what he thinks he knows.

Instead, he asks, "What do you propose we do about Ethel?"

"Ethel's already been taken care of." I settle back in my seat with a raised eyebrow. "What's the point of being a billionaire if you can't help people?"

"Money is not the solution for everything, and it's definitely not sustainable." He points out something that I already know. "Although I'm glad to hear you're spending it on other things besides…"

I stop him before he says something pretentious and asinine.

"Which is the reason I asked you here. Rori Colton's seat will be empty," I take a deep breath because now that it's out, now that I've said it, I can't take it back.

"What happened to not caring about politics?"

"Money runs out, but power is evergreen." I never wanted to be a politician, but the world continues to spin, and with it comes change.

"Or your term is up," Rausch points out ominously.

"Are you already saying I won't get re-elected?" I joke.

"Maybe you should have inferred I had confidence that you got elected in the first place." He raises his eyebrows at me, a hint of playful amusement on his face. This is what he wanted all along. Why shouldn't he be happy about it? He is the kingmaker after all.

Will he make a king out of me?

Politics is his playground, his pitch, and no one has the track record for wins that he does. If I want to do this, then I need him.

"So you think I have a chance?" I ask, my insecurities coming through, because I am well aware of my past and my present. I'm not a saint, and although everyone has skeletons in their closet, mine are, well, not flattering.

"You have the advantage of being Kerry Walker's son, and before you accuse me of being callous, I say this putting aside my own personal feelings. Now that he has passed, it gives you a certain advantage with the public. If you're worried about certain indiscretions, there are things that can be minimized, but nothing that we can't handle."

"Are those things Evangeline?" I inquire cautiously.

He shifts in his seat uncomfortably, and I already know the answer.

"What does she say about this?" he asks.

"That's for me to worry about."

"If it's your desire to bring her into this with you, I will do my best to protect her," he offers shockingly.

My first order of business is to pass the bar, and the rest will come.

"You should warn her about this," he offers. "Winning an election is nasty business."

"It's just Representative for a small district in Virginia." I shake my head.

"And Barrack Obama was once a senator for the thirteenth district of Illinois." He levels me with a stare.

"He was a Democrat." I raise my eyebrows.

He rests his arm against the back of the chair. "Virginia has voted for Democrats in presidential campaigns since 2008, and the only former confederate state to vote for Hillary Clinton over Donald Trump."

"This is information you just happen to have in your back pocket?" I jest.

He presses his lips together, and then I know. He gathered this information because my father was going to run.

"Well, then that's good news in my favor," I broach the subject of party lines.

Rausch smiles, not what I expected since my father was a

Republican. I expected him to give me a speech about following in my father's footsteps and losing voters.

"You're not disappointed?"

"Only if you lose," he offers. "But don't forget that we used to be called the Democratic Republican's." There's a gleam in his eyes.

I nod, sitting back in my chair, and twirling a pen between my fingers.

"I have a favor to ask," I say with caution, because asking for a favor comes with strings, and it's those strings that could make me very uncomfortable.

"Of course," Rausch laughs as if he was waiting for this. He places his hands on either side of the chair, his left hand gripping the edge like the Lincoln Memorial. Rausch might be made with the hardness of marble, but he's still just a man – and men still have a taste for revenge.

"How friendly are you with Senator Jonathan Langley?"

Rausch laughs. "Washington is a landscape that breeds chameleons. Friends can shift into enemies like the day shifts into night."

He folds his hands in his lap. "What are you after, Darren?"

"He can be a problem, as I'm sure you know."

"Let's not start this off with false pretense. He was a client of Evangeline's. If you want to bury him, then let's not pretend it's political."

I scowl. Of course he's right.

"Alright then."

"I'm sure you know the terms," he reminds me that nothing, not even information, is given freely.

I nod.

"Then what do you have in mind?"

27

I'm A Liability
Evangeline

*A*s I put welcome packages together, I'm still struck with the thought that some women are in such a hurry to leave that they don't even have time to pack necessities. Even though I've been doing this the past few months, I'm still affected. But I feel good. I have a sense of purpose that I'd been missing.

Once the bags have been filled, I sort the clothes. When I get to the box with blazers and skirts it brings a smile to my face, because this is the one thing I can say that I did myself. Bethany was in charge of monetary donations, which went mostly towards rent and insurance. I had the idea to call some of the clothing stores to see if they would be willing to donate professional clothing the women could use to go on interviews.

It's a wonderful feeling to empower someone to be able to care for themselves, because even though they have the safe house, it's only temporary.

While I hang up the clothes in the storage room, I hear a voice from behind me. "My mother spent a lot of time here."

Darren's standing in the doorway, one ankle casually crossed over the other. His dark locks are windswept, and he has a satisfied smile on his face. His shoulders are dusted with snow, and behind him through the front window I can see the snow falling.

"Patty told me."

Darren enters the room, looking around the small entryway and past the stairs that leads to the kitchen.

"What did she tell you?" Darren inquires, shoving his hands in the pockets of his overcoat and leaning over the table.

"She told me how Merrill used to help in the kitchen and serve meals," I smile.

Darren laughs. "She was great at hiring caterers, but cooking herself, no."

I laugh.

"Patty didn't say she was good at it. She said one time, Merrill spilled soup on her pants and had to borrow a pair of jeans from the closet here." I couldn't help my interest in knowing what Darren's mother was like. She seemed like such an interesting woman. I like hearing stories about her.

"I cannot imagine my mother wearing jeans." Darren raises his eyebrows, another laugh escaping his lips.

I finish folding the clothes while Darren explores a little more, looking at pictures on the wall, one of them taken when the house was first opened, and his mother stood on the front steps with the other volunteers.

"I've never been here," Darren admits, his voice laced with regret.

"Why not?" I ask softly.

An embarrassed smile passes over his face. "I guess I always had more important things to do."

"Like squandering your potential?" I tease.

"Something like that," he sighs.

I pull a container from the floor and hand it to him. Reluctantly he takes it and starts stacking the packages inside. When he finishes, I show him where to place it in the storage room, stacking it on the top shelf for me.

Darren reaches down and picks up a small teddy bear that must have fallen out of the bins. He looks at it before setting it back with the rest.

"Sometimes kids don't have time to grab their stuffed animals before they come here," I explain while closing the cabinets and flipping the lock back on. "It doesn't replace what they had to leave behind, but it makes them feel better."

"My mother never really discussed any of this with me," he admits, "but I guess I never really asked. It's not exactly dinner conversation."

I tilt my head in confusion.

"Discussing such things isn't proper dinner etiquette," he attempts to exaggerate how his mother would sound. "Did you ever feel like you were born into the wrong family?" he questions, forcing me to think of just how sad and lonely someone as exuberant as Darren felt being confined to proper dinner etiquette among other things.

"No." I push a stray piece of hair behind my ear. "Although I have wished I was."

Darren stares at me, and the confines of the storage unit are too small to contain our confessions.

"You can't choose the family you were born in, but you can choose the family that you belong in," he says.

"I don't think it works like that."

"Why not?" he challenges.

"Because it just doesn't."

His lips open slightly as if the words he wants to say are trying to find their way out, but then he presses his lips back together before he walks out of the storage room.

"Rori Colton's seat in the Fifth Congressional District is open," he declares, and it leaves me with a prickle of something more to come.

I have a feeling, but I ask anyway. "What does that mean, Darren?"

"I spoke with Rausch, and he's behind me…"

"Rausch?" I widen my eyes. "So you're telling me you want to run?"

"He's someone you want on your side politically," he explains. "And yes."

"Why would you do this?" I ask, and his face falls.

"I thought you'd be happy for me." He pinches his brows together. "Getting my life together and shit."

"I don't know why you would think that." I take my aggression out on breaking down the cardboard boxes to get them ready for the trash.

"Why are you so upset about this?"

"You can do whatever you want, Darren." I tuck the cardboard under my arm and stalk down the hallway through the kitchen where some of the volunteers are getting dinner ready.

Darren follows me into the alley where the trash bins are.

"I thought you'd be happy. I can help people like Ethel, make a real difference!" he raises his voice, and I let the heavy lid fall back into place.

I whirl around. "Is that why you gave me access to the money? I demand.

"Are you seriously asking me that?" Darren growls. "I already told you why I gave you the money."

I know what he said.

"It would be the best thing for you."

"You think I would be better off without you?" Darren levels me with his eyes.

"You of all people know what will happen." I try to walk around him, but he stops me.

We stare at each other, heaviness between us, his hand wrapped around my arm, holding me in place. "They will dig up things that should stay buried," I say quietly.

"That won't happen."

"You don't know that."

He releases my arm, but I stay in place.

"You could wait."

His eyes flare as soon as he catches my meaning.

"I would think you know me better by now," his voice is husky, the heat from his breath catching in the air before dissolving between us. Snowflakes settle in his dark hair.

"When I want something, I take it."

"I'm a liability, Darren."

He takes my chin between his fingers, tilting my head towards his, forcing me to look at him. It's not his hand that keeps me in place, but his eyes, the way he stares down at me as if he wants to either scold me or kiss me.

"You are *not* a liability, Evangeline."

"Wake up, Darren!" I throw my arms in the air. "You married a prostitute. You can't come back from that. I don't care who you have in your corner."

He grabs onto me tighter. "You have no idea what I'm capable of when it comes to you."

"Darren," I sigh.

He lets go of me, agitation vibrating off him. "I want to do something with my life." He runs a hand through his hair and turns away from me. "I have this last name that has been a burden most of my life, but it doesn't have to be."

His eyes glisten green, and tears threaten to freeze on his lashes until he blinks them back.

"This is something I can do and be really good at. I can feel it, Evan. I can feel it in my bones. Maybe I always have and that's why I ran from it, but I can't run anymore," he says with frustration, an internal argument that is ancient and weary.

I know he's capable of it, and seeing him now, on the verge of becoming something great, just makes it all the more bittersweet because he won't be anything as long as I'm in his life.

"What about the bar exam?" I ask.

"I take the bar next week and I've never been more ready for anything in my life. Do you trust me?" he pleads.

I want to say that I do, but that would be a lie. I can't even trust myself, especially not when he's looking at me the way a man does when he will pull the moon from the sky just to make you smile. But pulling the moon is the stuff of fairytales.

Fairytales I don't believe in.

"You just have to believe in me," he says quietly.

"I believe in you so much that I don't want to be the reason you don't succeed," I try to reason with him, but I can already see that reason won't work.

His expression softens. "Everything depends on passing the exam. One thing at a time, okay?"

I manage to nod my head, but I can't shake the uneasiness I feel inside.

I shiver against the cold and he takes the scarf from around his neck and places it over my head, still holding onto the ends as he pulls me close to him.

"I don't want to do this without you."

Then he tosses one of the ends of the scarf over my shoulder.

Instead of kissing my lips, he kisses the top of my head. I press my face into his jacket, getting lost in the smell of him. It reminds me of the lake house when things felt simple and I didn't have to worry about the future.

I know he would do everything he could to protect me... that's what I'm afraid of.

28

Superstitions
Darren

"You're distracting," I grumble from my seat at the kitchen island, a practice test in front of me for the second half of my Bar exam tomorrow.

"I'm not doing anything," she protests while reaching for a mug in the cabinet.

"You're doing that." I pull my glasses off and use them to motion towards her.

"This?" She reaches for another mug, causing her sweater to glide up her body and expose the underside of her breast.

"Evangeline," I warn.

This is playing with fire, and she knows it.

I pull in a deep breath because when she turns towards me, her lips pull into a pout and I my resolve disappears.

"Do you want me to fail?" I question, slipping my glasses back on. I only wear them to focus, the prescription not strong but helpful.

"You're not going to fail. You've spent the last week in the office barely paying attention to me," she accuses, setting a cup of coffee in front of me.

"You know why," I remind her.

"It doesn't make any sense to me."

"Professional athletes abstain from sex before a big game in order to pour all of that pent up energy into winning."

She places her hand on her hip and takes a sip of her coffee. "Are you calling yourself a professional athlete now?"

"Do you want me to go back to the office?" I threaten.

"I'll be a good girl," she promises, and I slap the pen down on the marble countertop.

When I look over my glasses she's smirking at me, and I wonder why I'm torturing myself. I want to fuck that smirk right off her face.

When her sweater slips down her shoulder, I almost crawl across the island to get to her.

"You realize how stupid this rule is," she states, holding the cup with both hands.

"Of course I realize how stupid it is," I grunt, flipping the page with more force than I intended, almost ripping it.

"You have a lot of pent-up frustration."

"You think?" I ask with a raised eyebrow. "I haven't fucked in a week. The last time that happened was when I was in high school and Kennedy Morgan popped my cherry. It took me a week to get up the nerve to do it again," I confess.

Evangeline laughs, the coffee spilling over the side of her mug as she jostles it.

"Kennedy Morgan? I'm surprised you still remember her name," she says between fits of laughter.

"Everyone remembers their first, especially when she's your friend's older sister."

She mouths the word wow.

The laughter dies, and I look up at her. "Who was your first?" I inquire, raising an eyebrow.

"Don't you have studying to do?"

"Apparently I'm taking a break."

"Well, don't let me distract you," she taunts.

"Uh uh," I cluck with my tongue, and stop her from leaving the kitchen. "I told you mine, now you tell me yours."

"Oh fine, Darren, but it's not as salacious as my friend's older brother crawling into bed with me during a sleepover."

"Get on with it then."

"A drive-in theater on a sweaty July night. The air conditioning didn't work in his truck, so we laid out a blanket in the bed." She shrugs.

"Well now I know where your fucking in public kink comes from."

I gather her up, holding down her arms so she can't swat at me. She struggles in my arms when I feel her phone vibrate in her back pocket and I release her. The wicked smile on her face is replaced with trepidation the minute she checks the screen.

"Hello?" she answers cautiously, as if she already knows the news is bad.

I watch as her eyes change like a shadow passing over them, closing up the blue skies with clouds. I try to wait patiently but she doesn't look at me – won't look at me.

"What happened?" I question, and her eyes snap up to mine.

She shakes her head, tears in her eyes, and hand over her mouth. I pull out a chair for her and she gladly takes it.

"She was doing fine. I just spoke with her. The medication was working. How?" she says into the phone.

"I just thought…" she doesn't finish her sentence, the tears overtaking her speech.

"Thank you, Maria. I'll let you know when I can get there." She looks down at me as I crouch down before her, resting my hands on her thighs.

"I'll be in touch." She hangs up the phone, placing it on the counter, and letting the tears fall freely now.

She's in pain, in desperate pain that I feel helpless to fix.

I do the only thing I can and take her into my arms, my shoulder collecting her tears as she once did for me.

"She had a stroke." She can barely get it out. "I knew there was a risk with her medication, but I never thought…" she doesn't finish. "I feel like this is my fault. I wanted more good days, and I was willing to sacrifice the possible side effects."

"It's not your fault, Evan. It's okay that you wanted more time with her," I try to console her.

"I know, it's just…" she falters. "I knew this was going to happen one day, I just wasn't prepared."

"No one ever is," I offer, and she looks at me understanding the meaning.

There aren't words to convey how helpless I feel right now, how I wish she didn't have to go through this. "I'm sorry. I'm so sorry," I whisper into her hair.

"I need to go back to Arizona," she declares.

"I'll go with you," I blurt out. "Let me go with you."

She pulls back just enough to look at me with watery blue eyes. "You have to take your exam tomorrow."

"I don't care about the exam," I blurt out in a rush.

"Don't say that. You worked so hard."

"I'll call the pilot, and he can have the plane ready to go as soon as I get out of my exam," I concede.

"You would do that for me?"

I run my thumb along her jaw. "There isn't anything I wouldn't do for you, Evangeline."

"I'm sorry," she apologizes.

"What could you possibly be sorry about?" I gather her face in my hands, wiping the tears from her cheek.

"Tomorrow is a big day for you and you need to study, but instead you're consoling me. I just… I don't…" she stammers.

"Evan," I force her to look at me. "It's fine. It's not your fault. I'll be fine."

She nods, wiping the remainder of the tears from her cheeks and pulls away from me.

"What do you need me to do? I can call funeral homes, order flowers, whatever you need," I speak a mile a minute.

"She had everything planned a while ago. There's nothing to do really except take care of her personal things when I get there," she explains.

I take in a deep breath. "What about your mother?" I inquire, feeling the tightness in my chest.

Her eyebrows furrow. "I'll have to call her," she confirms with a troubled tremble of her voice. "It's the right thing to do."

"I hate that you have to deal with this." I pull her back into me, running my palm gently over her back.

She wraps her arms around me, and I can feel the tears soak through my shirt, but I just press her tighter to me. I have never been the kind of person someone would turn to for comfort; the kind of person anyone would go to for support.

The feeling makes my chest expand and my heart swell, just as much as it aches for her. In this instance, I'm the strong one, and I'm only too eager to give back to her when she has given me so much.

"It's okay," I whisper into her hair. "It's gonna be okay."

29

Of All The Ways To Lose Someone

Evangeline

I can't sleep. Every time I do, I dream of Mimi. I close my eyes and see her room, the plain white sheets of her hospital bed, the extra fluffy pillows I got for her, and the afghan from home, so she'd be comfortable.

I toss and turn, trying to not to wake Darren because he has a big day today, and he needs his sleep. When he turns over and places his hand on the back of my head, I let him pull me against his chest.

"When my parents first died, I couldn't sleep," he discloses in a raspy voice that sounds like midnight. "Every time I closed my eyes, I kept seeing the helicopter. I would sit in the formal living room, because it was the only room that didn't hold a memory," he confesses. "I thought it would give me a dreamless sleep."

"Did it work?" I ask.

"No," he lets out a sigh. "Nothing worked."

"And now?"

"It doesn't keep me awake at night anymore. It takes time,

but you'll be able to sleep again. I promise," he cajoles in a comforting tone.

"She left me, Darren. The only person who ever truly cared about me… and she's gone," I admit, feeling terribly alone in the world, even though I'm engulfed in Darren's arms.

"Of all the ways to lose a person, death is the kindest," he laments. "She didn't leave you because she wanted to, Evan."

"I like it when you quote Emerson," I admit, tucking myself deeper into his chest.

"Then I shall give you an entire poem," he promises in a husky voice.

"You need to sleep," I tell him.

He shushes me and places a hand in my hair. I can feel his body settle deeper into the mattress, and I do the same.

I place my ear against his chest, and the faint beating of his heart comforts me. When he speaks, I feel the vibration throughout my body.

"Give all to love/obey thy heart/friends kindred days," he whispers with a sleepy voice that's rough and raw. I close my eyes.

"Leave all to love/yet, hear me, yet/one word more thy heart beloved," he continues.

"When half-gods go/The gods arrive." His voice is barely a whisper as he finishes the poem.

"You won't be any good for your exam if you don't go to sleep," I chastise him.

"I'll stay up as long as you need me."

"Why would you do that?"

He shifts his body to look down on me. "Do you really have to ask?"

I furrow my brows and lift my hand to his face. He hasn't shaved, and I run my fingers over the rough patch of hair along his jaw. His body trembles and I shake my head.

I don't think I can bear it if he says it.

"Darren," I start to say but he interrupts me.

"All this time, you have to know," he admits.

"You shouldn't, you really shouldn't."

"It's not something I can control. I didn't choose it," he whispers, but his voice is still resolute. "I didn't choose to fall in love with you, but now that I have, I wouldn't change it. I *can't* change it, so don't ask me to."

I don't know what to say and I don't know how to feel, so I break his rule and reach for him, placing a tentative kiss on his lips.

I kiss him until he yields and kisses me back. When he does, it's with a fervor that rivals the turmoil inside of me. His mouth is hot and seeking, but it's different, slower and deeper. It's the way he opens for me, and the slow languorous strokes of his tongue that makes me believe he would be content to kiss me all night until one or the other of us falls asleep.

I pull him closer, wrapping my leg around him as if I could crawl inside. My body is a charged wire, and all he's done is run his hand over my hip to pull me in closer. I kiss down his jaw to the hollow of his neck, listening to his ragged breaths and taking in the faded scent of his cologne. I want him to make me forget, just for today, because I'm not ready for reality… even though I know it's inevitable. I want to remember him, to have him fuck me so hard that he'll leave an imprint on me.

Pulling on the waistband of his boxers, I'm surprised when he grabs my wrists and stops me.

Shadows are cast across his face from the window as he looks at me thoughtfully. At a time when I don't want him to show restraint, he does.

"Darren," I breathe.

He lifts my arms over my head and rolls me over, pushing my back into the mattress as his body rests on top of mine. The wind is knocked out of me, sending a pulse straight down the center of my body. He's looking at me as if there's a war going on inside his mind and I squirm, wanting to touch him, but my hands are restrained.

He's hard against me, and I lift my hips to meet his, watching his lips part as he exhales.

He drags his cock along my center, the pressure grounding and sweet. Even though our clothes are still on, it makes me needy, wanting more of him – always wanting more of something that is just short of within my grasp. He cups my face and kisses me while I wrap my arms around his shoulders, pulling him closer.

Yesterday was playful, trying to get him to break his superstition, but now I feel guilty, tempting him because I'm being selfish.

"What happened to your superstition?" I ask him.

"I love you more than any superstition, and I'll take the consequences because it would be worth it. *You* are worth it." He works his way down my body, sliding my panties off and I whimper. It's not just because his mouth and his breath whisper along my skin, but because I can't bear his words, what he feels for me. I'm not worthy.

He presses kisses to the inside of my thigh that make me shake. By the time he works his way to my mouth, I'm a mess. Everything about him is slow and deliberate, unmistakably tender to the point that it makes me want to cry. When he finally pushes inside me, I'm so needy that I'm ready to fall apart.

Sex with Darren has always been easy. Fucking him in a coat check closet, on a piano, or even in the same room as the Declaration of Independence. As easy as breathing.

Making love to him just might break me.

30

Punch To The Gut
Darren

*B*ouncing on the balls of my feet, I stand at the curb of the Washington Convention Center where I just finished a grueling six hours of writing essays on family law and conflicts. I wait impatiently for Bailey to pull through traffic so we can be on our way to the airport. I packed everything before I left, made arrangements on my way to the exam.

Excitement has taken hold of me when all logic says I should be ready to pass out because the Bar exam sucks the life out of you.

But I feel good.

It was the fear of failing and not being able to step out of my father's shadow that kept me grounded for so long, but right now, I feel like flying.

I nailed it.

I can feel it in my bones, and all I want to do is take Evangeline's face in my hands and kiss her because I feel like I can set the world on fire.

I check my phone, seeing a few texts from Alistair wishing

me luck, and then another one with a meme of a celebrity toasting a glass of champagne with the caption that says, *cheers old fellow, you just passed the Bar exam.*

I press dial and he picks up immediately. "I'm renting out The Tombs tonight so we can celebrate!" he yells into the phone. "Even though you didn't do the same for me when I passed my series seven," he mentions with an accusatory tone.

"Okay, first of all, the series seven is a three-hour exam that any buffoon can pass, and the bar exam is a two-day event on how to acclimate yourself to torture techniques," I yell into the phone. "And second, I won't know if I passed for two months."

"Shit, I'll have to call you back," Alistair relents in a dejected tone. "I wonder if I can get my deposit back. Oh, who cares? And by the way, I resent your tone. I studied very hard for that exam."

He sounds offended enough for me to feel bad about calling him a buffoon. "I'm sorry, you know I didn't mean that. It's been a very long day. Evangeline's grandmother died," I explain.

"Shit, that's awful, I'm sorry."

"We're flying to Arizona right away."

"Arizona is the seventh circle of hell," Alistair groans.

"When have you been to Arizona?" I inquire.

"A festival a few years ago when you ditched me to go to Belize with that model."

"I don't remember that."

"Convenient."

While Alistair blabbers, I check the curb again, but there's no sign of Bailey. Figures today of all days there would be some kind of traffic jam, and I can only hope it's not a Presidential motorcade.

"I told her I loved her," I interrupt him in a rush.

There's silence on the other end, which is rare for Alistair.

"Hello?" I say into the phone before holding it away from my ear to check if he hung up on me.

"Yeah, yeah, I'm still here," he says.

"Shouldn't come as a shock. Even you saw it," I remind him. "I couldn't let her go back to Arizona without telling her, Alistair."

"Because you were afraid she wouldn't come back?" he inquires, sparking a pebble of insecurity.

"Of course not, why would you think that?"

"She has no reason to fulfill the contract now, Darren. You gave her access to the money." Alistair is not supposed to be the voice of reason, but here I am, doubting myself.

"I gave her access to it because it was the right thing to do. I didn't want to hold her to something that should have never been a condition in the first place." I run a hand through my hair and look up at the grey sky.

I hear Alistair sigh on the other end and I stop breathing, my heart no longer pressing against my chest with vigor.

"She wouldn't," as soon as I say it, I can feel my heart seize like an electric shock trying to bring it back to life.

She didn't say it back last night, but I felt it in the way she kissed me. I felt it in the way she gave her whole self to me. At least that's what I had thought. When I left this morning, she was still asleep, and I didn't want to wake her. Perhaps I thought if she opened her eyes and didn't look back at me the way I was looking at her, it might break me.

I needed to get my head in the game because I broke all my rules.

Stupid rules about sex before an exam.

Reckless rules about falling in love.

"Look, I know how it sounds, but you know Evan, she's never been interested in the money. It was so she could pay for her grandmother's care, and well, her grandmother passed away."

"I thought I knew her, too," he offers sympathetically, and his tone makes me uneasy. He knows something I don't.

"Did she take the money?" I question, gripping the phone tightly.

"You know I can't tell you that. It's against the law."

"Since when are you ever worried about walking a straight line?" I ask, angrily.

"Darren, don't do this to yourself," he pleads.

"I'm standing on this fucking curb and she's not here. I need to know," I practically beg, knowing there is a tremor in my voice that I can't hide.

"Darren…" he tries to reason with me.

"Did she take the fucking money?!"

Alistair sighs and I know he's given in. "I got the liquidation order this morning."

"Fuck!" I want to punch something, to throw my phone into the concrete sidewalk, but I don't. That was the old Darren.

"Darren? Darren!" is all I hear before hanging up the phone, just as Bailey pulls up at the curb.

I yank the car door open before Bailey can get out, knowing she's not in there but still feeling shocked when the backset is empty.

"Where is she?"

Bailey gives me a sympathetic look. "I took Mrs. Walker to the airport this morning."

I slide into the back seat and slam the door.

"I'm sorry, boss," Bailey offers. "I thought you knew."

I rub my chin and look out the window as we pull into traffic. "No, I did not know."

I should be angry at him for taking orders from her, for letting her leave, but it's not his fault. He was just doing his job. I was gonna let her leave before, but things are different now. I fucking told her I loved her.

Jesus!

"Take me home."

She left and took the money.

It's like a punch to the gut.

Maybe I should have seen it coming.

As soon as we pull alongside the curb, I shove the door open and bound up the porch, into the house, taking the stairs two at a time, only to find the guest room, *her room*, empty. As if I thought I would find anything different.

The only thing left behind is my Georgetown t-shirt, neatly folded on the bed, with her ring sitting on top of it.

31

His Queen Of Ruin
Evangeline

Through the airplane window is the familiar deep browns, reds, and golds of the mountains looking like a Maynard Dixon painting – muted but distinct and inexplicably Arizona. There is nothing more beautiful, and yet I can't appreciate it.

Sporadic blue lakes dot the desert landscape, and in the distance, the hazy outline of the Phoenix skyline spreads out like an oasis. I can almost see the heat rising from the steel and concrete.

Home.

Trepidation settles deep in my stomach, almost making me feel sick the closer we get. I could go anywhere, be anyone – change myself like a chameleon, but there are things unfinished, and one of those is my obligations to Mimi. All of this was for her, and I don't regret one thing because she had a good life – ignorant of my sacrifices, and ignorant of the ones my mother *didn't* make.

Some might not understand my choices, think that she wasn't worth it, but she was the only family I really had. She made me feel safe, enveloped in the familiar scent of her perfume – heavy and floral; a perfume I will never smell again, and with it any sense of family or belonging.

I settle back in my seat, focusing on the book in my hands as I flip the page, nearing the end and knowing that when I do, I will go back to the beginning again. Reading these words has been my salvation for the entire plane ride. Without them, I would be vulnerable to my own thoughts that creep in even now – Darren's wolfish smile, his confession of love crushing me like deep waters and stealing my breath – knowing that I would leave while he said it.

The stewardess appears from the galley just in time before I spiral too far. "Mrs. Walker, we'll be landing soon."

I try my best to smile politely, but inside, my emotions swirl like a cyclone. I close the book, running my finger over the cover before slipping it into my purse.

I tell myself that I made the right decision, that he'll be better off without me. In time, he'll realize it was just a mirage, a temporary oasis.

I can't pretend that I won't be his downfall.

His Queen of Ruin.

Find out what happens next in the exciting final book in the Kingmaker Trilogy, State of Union, paperback available on Paula's direct shop, Barnes & Noble, and Amazon. eBook available at your favorite retailer and Paula's direct shop.

Read on for an excerpt of State of Union.

STATE OF UNION EXCERPT

DARREN

"*I* don't know who any of these people are," I gesture as I walk through the campaign head-quarters, passing by a blue and white banner with the name Walker hanging on the wall.

"Do you think your father knew the names of each volunteer on his staff? He had better things to do," Rausch says as I sit down behind the desk.

Over the past few months, the campaign has ramped up from just a couple of volunteers to a now-bustling room with the shrill sound of phones ringing. I tap my chin with a pen while I watch through the glass partition, and I can't help but think of my mother spending all her time organizing the volunteers of my father's campaign. She knew all their names, even if my father didn't. He relied on her for those things so that he could concentrate on the campaign. Granted, his campaign wasn't for a small district in Virginia, but this is my diving platform where I can test out the waters, learn from mistakes, and hopefully make a difference, too.

I brush my thumb over the place where my wedding ring used to be, now not as foreign with it off as if was at first.

I'm only slightly aware of Rausch's voice in the background. "I have you on the schedule to speak at the VFW hall on Thursday. I think…"

"I'm not my father," I abruptly say, and Rausch stops.

I set the pen down and look across the desk at him. "It's not a statewide campaign. The problem with Rori Colton is that he didn't know people like Ethel and the problems they faced. It made it easier for him to vote down a Bill that could have saved them, instead of saving the state money," I declare.

Looking back into the heart of the office, I state, "It's a small southern district of Virginia. I need to know people's names, starting with the volunteers."

Rausch sits back in his chair and nods. He tries to hide the smile on his face, but the tilt of his lips tells me that he's proud of me, even if he doesn't always agree with me. I stand up and Rausch follows as I head into the bullpen, making my way around the room and introducing myself as if these people hadn't been working for me for the last month.

During my father's campaign I would have to put on a smile, shake hands, and pretend to enjoy small talk while pushing my father's agenda. I find that my smile comes easily, naturally, even if deep down I'm still nursing a wound. Perhaps this is what has kept me going the last couple months – throwing myself into the campaign.

The small bell at the top of the door jingles, a leftover from the hardware store that used to occupy this space on main street. Ethel walks in, her crocheted handbag tucked under her arm as she looks around the space, her eyes finally meeting mine.

Ethel eyes the space skeptically. "Looks like a bunch of pomp and circumstance to me."

"Are you looking to volunteer?" I tease and raise a challenging eyebrow.

"I figure you could use someone with my sunny disposition," she says sarcastically, and I can't help but smile.

"Well then, I have a spot for you right over here." I lead the way to a desk near the windows.

Rausch approaches. "Is this the famous Ethel?" he asks.

Ethel places a hand on her hip and looks up at him as he towers over her short frame. "I don't know about famous, but whatever you've heard," she pauses, "is probably true."

Rausch laughs and looks over at me with approval. Apparently; Ethel can win over anyone.

"Where's that pretty wife of yours?" she asks, and it's like a pierce to my heart.

Before I can make an excuse, Rausch interrupts.

"Angie," he calls over to the woman that's been training the volunteers. "This is Ethel, and she would like to volunteer."

"People say I got a voice like honey, so if you want to put me on the phones, that's fine with me," she declares to Angie.

I give Rausch a thankful nod and retreat to my office. I have reference material to go over before my meeting at the VFW hall.

"Excuse me," a young man says from the doorway. "Are you Darren Walker?"

I nod.

He drops the envelope on my desk and says, "You've been served."

I don't even notice him leaving, because in front of me is an envelope from a law office in Phoenix, Arizona. My stomach drops while I rip the envelop open to find divorce papers from Evangeline.

Pulling off my tie, I throw it across the room with an unceremonious affect because I should have expected this, but I'm still thrown off kilter. It's been three months, and I can blame the campaign for keeping me busy… but the truth is I couldn't bring myself to draw up the papers. Apparently she has not been so restricted by time.

"Don't forget about the fundraising event tonight,"

Rausch says as he enters my office. He sees my tie lying on the ground and picks it up, and when he places it on the desk he looks at the papers.

"You can gloat if you want to," I tell him angrily. "You got what you wanted, right?"

"If you want me to say that Evangeline leaving was the best thing for your campaign, then fine, but that doesn't mean I'm happy about seeing you in pain."

I scoff.

"You can think what you want, Darren, but what I said to you before was the truth. If you wanted her with you on the campaign, I would do everything to protect her," he says with sincerity.

If there is one thing I know about Rausch, it's that he keeps his word.

I lift my eyes from the papers. "Well, it seems she didn't want to be a part of this life after all."

Rausch lets out a breath. "You can sit here and stare at those papers, or you can pull yourself together and win this election."

Read State of Union now. Paperback available on Paula's direct shop, Barnes & Noble, and Amazon. eBook available at your favorite retailer and Paula's direct shop.

PAULADOMBROWIAK.COM

ALSO BY PAULA DOMBROWIAK

THE BLOOD & BONE SERIES

A Steamy Rockstar Romance series

BLOOD AND BONE (BOOK 1)

Two days. One Interview. Twenty-five years of Rock 'n Roll. Telling his story might just repair past relationships and ignite new ones.

BREATH TO BEAR (BOOK 2)

These chains that weigh me down, my guilt I wear like a crown, SHE is my Breath to Bear

BONDS WE BREAK (BOOK 3)

To have and to hold from this day forward - to love and to cherish, till death do us part - and these are the bonds we break.

BOUND TO BURN (BOOK 4)

Love has a way of blazing through you like poison, leaving you breathless but still wanting more.

BLOOD & BONE BOXSET PLUS BONUS NOVELLA

All four books in the Blood & Bone series plus a bonus novella.

Blood & Bone legacy, bonus novella, give you a glimpse twenty years in the future through the eyes of their children.

This is their legacy.

Already read the series but just want the bonus novella?

Grab it exclusively on my SHOP

BLOOD & BONE LEGACY, A BONUS NOVELLA

STANDALONES

BEAUTIFUL LIES

I own the boardroom. He owns the stage. We were never meant to be together, but when somethings forbidden, it only makes you want it more.

A forbidden, reverse age gap romance

KINGMAKER SERIES

A Steamy, Marriage of Convenience, Political Romance Trilogy

King of Nothing, Book 1

Queen of Ruin, Book 2

State of Union, Book 3

ABOUT THE AUTHOR

Paula Dombrowiak grew up in the suburbs of Chicago, Illinois but currently lives in Arizona. She is the author of Blood and Bone, her first adult romance novel which combines her love of music and imperfect relationships. Paula is a lifelong music junkie, whose wardrobe consists of band T-shirts and leggings which are perpetually covered in pet hair. She is a sucker for a redeemable villain, bad boys and the tragically flawed. Music is what inspires her storytelling.

If you would like a place to discuss Paula's books, you can join her Facebook Reader Group **Paula's Rock Stars Reader Group**

You can always find out more information about Paula and her books on her website

PAULADOMBROWIAK.COM

You can also purchase eBooks, signed paperbacks, audiobooks, and multi-book bundles on her direct shop.

PAYHIP.COM / PAULADOMBROWIAKBOOKS

ACKNOWLEDGMENTS

I could not have written this book without the support of my family. Thank you so much for always being there for me, and for allowing me the space to create.

To my beautiful alpha reader's, Nattie (a.k.a. Poopsie) and Mishie, I wouldn't be who I am without your friendship and this book would not be possible without your support and incredible feedback. I'm not sure how I got so lucky to call you both friends but you're stuck with me for life.

To Lena Moore, you beautiful soul. Thank you for reading and providing your insight into Darren and Evangeline's story. I treasure our daily check-in's and words of encouragement.

To my editor Dayna Hart, who loves to cut my word count but I'm not mad at her. She makes my stories better.

Thank you to Katy Nielsen for proofreading. You are and always will be the one to find and fix all my errors, especially homophones. I may leave a few in there for you on purpose, just to keep you on your toes.

To my street team, thank you for sharing all my teasers on your social media because it makes a huge difference for this little indie author. Thank you for your friendship, and the laughs. I love you girls!!!

To all the Bookstagrammers, Bloggers, and Booktokers out there who have supported me, shared my posts, reviewed my books, and reached out to me, thank you, thank you, thank you! Word of mouth is huge! Your love of books astounds me, and I am so grateful to be a part of such a wonderful book community.

To my ARC readers, thank you from the bottom of my heart for reading and providing your honest review. Reviews are so important - especially for us little indie authors.

Last, but certainly not least, to my readers!!! I can't tell you how much you mean to me. In my heart I've always been a writer, but you make it real. I am always touched when readers reach out to me to say how much they connected with my characters. I strive to write from the heart, create characters that are real and flawed, and portray them in the most sensitive way possible. I hope you continue on this journey with me. Thank you for your support!

www.ingramcontent.com/pod-product-compliance
Ingram Content Group UK Ltd.
Pitfield, Milton Keynes, MK11 3LW, UK
UKHW041411210325
5105UKWH00014B/63